THE TRAGEDY AT FREYNE

Anthony Gilbert

Spitfire Publishers

Copyright © 2023 Spitfire Publishers LTD

First published in 1927 by W. Collins Sons & Company, London and by Lincoln MacVeagh, The Dial Press, New York, also in 1927. This edition published by Spitfire Publishers LTD in 2023.

TO
G.K.M.
WHO IS PARTIAL TO A CORPSE

CONTENTS

Title Page
Copyright
Dedication
About 'The Tragedy at Freyne'   1
Chapter 1 The Artist at Home   4
Chapter 2 The Mystery of the Locked Door   16
Chapter 3 The Step in the Night   33
Chapter 4 What the Library Revealed   50
Chapter 5 The Spinning of the Net   62
Chapter 6 The Verdict   77
Chapter 7 A New Trail   86
Chapter 8 The Anonymous Letter   99
Chapter 9 The Man of Mystery   106
Chapter 10 The Woman in Black   117
Chapter 11 The Woman in Black   124
Chapter 12 Nemesis   136
Chapter 13 A Journalistic Stunt   144
Chapter 14 The Man with the Red Beard   154
Chapter 15 The Woman in Black Again   172
Chapter 16 A Race Against Time   177
Chapter 17 The End of the Trail   191

Chapter 18 The Scales Adjusted

ABOUT 'THE TRAGEDY AT FREYNE'

When Sir Simon Chandos is found poisoned in his library, with a confession in front of him and a phial of morphia tablets on the table at his side, suicide is the obvious deduction. This is a dreadful shock to the members of the house party gathered in his picturesque old Norman country house, Freyne Abbey. But the discovery of a trivial discrepancy, by one of the guests, turns the suspicion in the direction of murder, and from that slight clue the amateur detective, Scott Egerton, unravels the web of an exceptionally brilliant and cold-blooded plot...

About the Author

Anthony Gilbert was one of four pseudonyms adopted by Lucy Beatrice Malleson, the English novelist who wrote over seventy detective and crime novels between 1925 and 1972. From the age of seventeen, she wrote verse and short pieces for *Punch* and various literary weeklies. Her first crime novel *The Man Who Was London* was published in 1925 under the name of J. Kilmeny Keith. She also wrote as Anne Meredith and Lucy Egerton. Malleson settled on the Anthony Gilbert pen name for her most popular literary creation, earthy, pugnacious, Cockney lawyer-detective Arthur G. Crook, who starred in over fifty novels. She was an early member of the prestigious Detection Club. She valued her privacy and for many years successfully concealed her identity as the writer of the Gilbert novels, even publishing her memoir, *Three-a-Penny*, under a pseudonym. It was recently reissued under her real name and was a BBC Radio 4 'Book of the Week'. She lived most of her life in London and never married. She died in 1973.

Praise for 'The Tragedy at Freyne'

'An unusually well told mystery tale'
New York Times

'A very good tale'
Boston Transcript

'Skilfully woven… makes good reading'
The Spectator

'Very mysterious and demands – and deserves – close attention on the part of the reader'
Times Literary Supplement

Praise for Anthony Gilbert

'Unquestionably a most intelligent author. Gifts of ingenuity, style and character drawing'
The Sunday Times

'Arthur Crook is a lawyer-sleuth worth meeting'
New York Times

'His stories, like his detective, Mr Crook, have vitality with decent and credible characters and, detection-wise, fair play'
Times Literary Supplement

'Careful in craftsmanship, scrupulously fair, more than well-written, Anthony Gilbert's novels show the unsensational type of detective story at its best'
The Daily Telegraph

'Anthony Gilbert is a master not only of the craft of the crime story, but also of the creation of character and atmosphere'
Irish Independent

'Mr Gilbert writes extremely well'
E.C. Bentley

'Anthony Gilbert has real descriptive power'
E.R. Punshon

CHAPTER 1 THE ARTIST AT HOME

I

The tragic death of Simon Chandos, occurring as it did just as he was entering into his kingdom, was bound to attract a good deal of attention. Subsequent events made it a *cause célèbre*. Fame had come to him late. He was, at the time of his death, fortynine, and his name was only just beginning to gain recognition even in artistic circles He had exhibited very little, because of that passion for perfection that tormented him, and would compel him, after months of unremitting labour, to scrape out a whole canvas and begin again. In addition to this, he was extraordinarily shy, chiefly, I believe, on account of his personal appearance. Certainly he was the ugliest man I have ever seen. There is an ugliness in men that appeals to women, but it was not his type. He was a shambling, inhuman figure, moving with a leaning-forward pose of body that suggested the ape; his head was finely-moulded, but the features were too large and heavy. The nose and mouth were a throw-back to monkey ancestors, though the eyes betrayed the mystic. He was seldom completely at ease, and clothes never became him gracefully. But his hands were beautiful: I have never seen their like. One had to see him at work to forget his physical disabilities. Then, he was transformed; a shining, spiritual Simon Chandos became apparent, blotting out the grotesqueries of the man, his harsh features, the clumsiness of his powerful limbs.

I imagine that it was this super-sensitiveness that kept him celibate for so long. But shortly after the Armistice he announced his engagement to my cousin, Catherine Armley. The news came to me as something of a shock. To begin with, Chandos was forty-four, worn by labour and disappointment and a certain nervousness noticeable in men who differ in any way from their fellows, while Catherine was a beautiful woman of eight-and-twenty, with any number of men at her feet. Besides, I had always thought she was more or less in love with her penniless, happy-go-lucky neighbour, Rupert Dacre, whom we had both known in childhood. He was a handsome fellow before the war got hold of him, brown as a gypsy, with Irish eyes and an Irish mind. One heard queer tales of his doings; personally, I didn't think he carried much ballast, and presumably Catherine thought the same, for within five months of the engagement she married Chandos. I was the best man, and for some hours before the ceremony I didn't think I should ever get the fellow as far as the church. He sweated like a nervous horse, but Catherine's calmness reassured him.

I went away from civilisation the following week, and I didn't hear much of the Chandoses, just a name in a letter from home sometimes, or an occasional note from the man himself waiting for me in some outlandish station I had told him I should visit. He said little of his home life, concentrating on his work and the condition of affairs in England, and it wasn't till some years later that I realised how tragically the whole thing had turned out. I think his ugliness had a good deal to do with it. Catherine was one of these unhappy women whom anything unlovely or inharmonious hurts like a wound. She might, and probably did, concentrate on the undoubted beauty of his work and of the mind that had conceived it, but the time came when it was obvious even to him what she endured when he took her in his arms, touched her even. At all events, when I came back four years later, they were occupying separate rooms. Chandos was absorbed in his painting. Dacre was staying there, and Catherine devoted a good deal of her time to him.

After that, I saw no more of either of them until the day of Chandos' death.

I had been back in London no more than an hour, and had found at my club a two-day old letter from him, inviting me down to Freyne.

"Come if you can,"—he wrote—"There may be one or two people here, since Rosemary has just celebrated her majority. But they need not trouble you, and I shall be glad of a little company."

The last words struck me as ominous, and I wired immediately that I would be coming down that afternoon. Coming back into the smoking-room I was accosted by a fellow called Philpotts whom I had known during the war.

"Come into port to take in coal?" he suggested.

"I'm going down to Freyne this afternoon," I told him.

"How long have you been back?"

"An hour and a half. It's a considerable time. Both Eve and Helen of Troy managed to wreck the world in less."

"They were women," returned Philpotts gloomily. "There's no end to the things women can do. Adam and Paris left alone wouldn't have accomplished much. But go down to Freyne by all means. I fancy your pal, Chandos, needs you."

"What's wrong," I asked quickly.

"Met him in town a week ago," Philpotts explained, "never saw a fellow looking more ghastly."

"Overdoing it, I expect."

Philpotts shook his massive head. "More than that. There was a woman with him...."

"What of it?" I asked coldly.

"I know, I know; rotten bad taste and all that, but Chandos is now a national acquisition. And, believe me, I'm a judge of women. (He certainly ought to have been.) That was a wrong 'un if ever I saw one. She's got her claws pretty deep into the poor devil and he can't get out. He knows it and so does she. More than just money, too. A fellow with his means doesn't turn gray even for a four-figure cheque."

"What the devil are you driving at?"

"It's occurred to me," he returned apologetically, "heard of it before—magazines, Sunday papers, National Education Authorities—some woman connected with his early life perhaps. Got him on a string and is biting his ear like blazes."

"This isn't the Lyceum," I reminded him.

"Perhaps not. But life can be damn well like a Lyceum melodrama sometimes. Suppose he married this woman in his twenties, thought her dead, and now she reappears like a ghost in black, and bleeds him white to save his wife's good name?"

I cursed him for an imaginative flapper with a vocabulary it had taken me years to accumulate. And he answered not a word. The remembrance of his silence haunted me throughout the journey to Freyne.

II

I was met at the station by Rosemary St Claire, Chandos' ward, who had to some extent filled the place of the children Catherine hadn't given him. She had dumped herself upon him at the age of sixteen after escaping from a villa in Penge where a dissenting aunt had brought her up on the Decalogue and a book of Christian principles. Since then she had alternated between London and Freyne.

She was, as always, aglow with *joie de vivre*. As she drove me back, taking all the corners on two wheels, and narrowly avoiding fowl-murder every time the road twisted, I asked her who was at Freyne.

"Rupert," she said briefly, and frowned. I frowned too. Dacre should have been too much of a man to be at Chandos' house these days, all things considered.

"The devil!" I muttered, and "It is the devil," Rosemary agreed. "It's worrying Simon to death. Rupert's worse than ever."

"About Catherine?"

"Of course."

"Then why . . . ?"

"I don't know. Simon's dreadfully bothered about it. He sits for hours doing nothing. Still, he was like that before Rupert came. Something's terribly wrong. I'm glad you've come, Alan. You'll help him."

"I doubt it," I murmured.

"Catherine's odd, too," Rosemary went on, "Freyne's like a mental hospital just now—everyone nervous and jumpy."

"What's wrong with Catherine?"

"Rupert, of course. I believe she's been in love with him from the beginning. She watches him when she thinks he isn't looking. She's afraid, and so's Simon, of what's going to happen to them all. Even strangers must see how it is with her."

"Are there many strangers?" Poor devil of a Chandos! In his own house, too!

"There's one man you'll like—a man called Bannister. He's travelled everywhere and seen everything and is frightfully clever and polished and all that."

"Where did you meet him?" I asked discourteously.

"At somebody's dance. He dances beautifully. After that I met him here and there, and when I said I should be at Freyne this weekend he said he knew the history of the Abbey and so forth, so I asked him to come down. I thought he'd be company for Catherine. I didn't know about Rupert then."

"Not for you?"

Rosemary blushed. "There's a man called Egerton," she began, turning the car rather neatly through the carriage gates. "And of course there's Miss Dennis. I believe she knows something."

"Concerning . . . ?"

"Whatever it is that's breaking Simon's heart. She's always been odd and mysterious, but now she sits and looks at him, follows him about, almost tries to ward the rest of us off."

The blush had faded: she was thinking of Simon Chandos. But I was thinking of the woman in black who had followed him to London, and mine were the darker thoughts of the two.

III

The library at Freyne is set to the right of the hall, under a pair of crossed swords that came, the one from Flodden Field, and the other from Naseby. I turned thither as the door closed behind us, knowing that Chandos would be there at such an hour. But out of the shadows round me rose a darker shadow barring my way. Rosemary's first fear was justified, that there was something strange about Simon Chandos, and that Althea Dennis knew it, and wanted to keep the rest of us away.

She was a dark, secretive woman of about five-and-thirty, sullen-lipped and swarthy, with a face like a partially clouded mirror, so that even her jealousy only revealed her moods to a certain degree. Today she was openly hostile, as she faced us, hating us for her dependent position, fierce and bitter.

"Sir Simon is engaged," she flung out at us, standing squarely in the doorway, her arms out-spread to keep us back, "he does not wish to be disturbed. Lady Chandos is in the smaller drawing-room."

Rosemary for an instant was taken aback. Then she recovered herself after the manner of those accustomed to give commands and said. "He is waiting for Mr Ravenswood. You misunderstand him, Miss Dennis."

A rush of dark blood gave Miss Dennis a wild, scarcely-human look. "I?" she cried passionately, "I *know*. It's you—you who don't understand. Will none of you ever let him rest?"

But as we moved forward, the door behind her opened and Chandos' exhausted voice said, "That you, Alan? I thought I heard your voice. Come in."

Miss Dennis turned away sharply, furious at her humiliation. "Thank you, Miss Dennis," he went on. "Rosemary, tell Catherine, will you, that Alan and I will be along directly?"

When the library door shut I faced my host, and my heart turned sick with apprehension. For he had lost that fire of enthusiasm that had always warmed him hitherto, even in his hours of blackest disillusion. He made me think of a fire that has burned fiercely for a long time and suddenly falls into gray ash.

"Tell me," I bade him, "about Rosemary. Has she really made up her mind?"

"She has," said Chandos. "I hope to God it will be all right. Her happiness is about the one thing left for me to stake on now. And she'll never be held by cast-iron conventions."

"She will not," I agreed, "but she'll cut her losses. She's better at that than any woman I know."

We were both silent a moment, remembering things that had happened to Rosemary St Claire during the past five years, and how gallantly she had met them all.

"Who's the man?" I thought to ask, when I had done remembering.

"Young Egerton—son of the reformer. Mad as a hatter, but my God! sincere. Francis of Assisi would have loved him—the father, I mean."

"And the boy?"

"He's taken it badly. He's got his father's brains. But it isn't as easy as falling off a log, marrying a girl like Rosemary. More like trying to hold the wind in your cap. Come up to tea now, and we'll talk later. There are divers things to discuss—including my will. But that can wait."

As I followed him up the stairs he seemed to me the loneliest creature I had ever seen, and I joined myself to the galaxy of people at Freyne who tasted fear—Chandos, Catherine, Rosemary, Dacre, Miss Dennis and I.

But if Chandos made me start with apprehension, Catherine left me dumb. That air of girlhood that had rested so evanescently on her had passed. She was a woman of five-and-thirty, and looked it. But like some plants whose second blooming is more exquisite than the first rapture, so was her mature loveliness more perfect than the charm of her youth. Her great gray eyes still smiled, that aloof secret smile, and she gave an impression of something faintly golden burning through the pervading whiteness of her dress. She resembled some wonderful picture of the Madonna, with Chandos for the poor devil of a penitent kneeling to kiss her garment's hem.

But he didn't kneel there alone. On the farther side of the room Dacre sat, his handsome face, badly scarred by war, set in a dark, sullen mask, his black eyes fixed on her. There was a menace in that silent, passionate, unceasing devotion. During the hour I spent in the drawing-room he sat there, stroking a Sealyham dog, who clearly loved him, watching Catherine's slightest movement. Whenever she spoke to him, which was seldom, he became a peculiar dead white, and the irregular scar he had brought back from Arras, that ran across his forehead, disappearing into his dark hair above the right eye, glowed like a red-hot poker.

I sat down by him and began to talk, hoping to relieve both his embarrassment and Catherine's. He answered me bitterly. I let him ramble on, and presently he became illuminating.

"War," he exclaimed, "makes a fellow realise that now he's either got to be a pirate, grabbing everything within reach, whether it belongs to him or not, or else he can go under. There's no third alternative."

That summed up his attitude. Such scruples as he would have experienced ten years ago at the thought of stealing from a man who was his friend had been withered by the cold blast of hunger and loneliness. Now he would take anything Catherine gave him.

I began to envy Philpotts his knowledge of women. I was all at sea. Here was Catherine discarding a man like Chandos for a neurotic, fear-saturated devil like Dacre, who could appeal to nothing but her compassion. And when I looked across the room I saw that Rosemary, who had had fine men and true in her retinue during the last three years, had chosen something flawlessly-dressed, painfully precise, something that looked as if it had just been taken out of a band-box. As a drawing-room ornament Scott Egerton was irreproachable; as a member of the least democratic body on this earth, the British House of Commons, he was typical, but as the husband of Rosemary, eager, impulsive Rosemary, who was like quicksilver to your touch, and could pass in an hour through the whole gamut of the human emotions—at that thought I shuddered as one shudders to see a wild thing locked into a gilded cage. He had his points, of course; he was well enough to look at, but Rosemary would ask for something more from a husband than that. He ought to have been swept off his feet, instead of preserving that air of cool detachment. He was the type that plans out life in cold blood and makes a cold-blooded triumph of the business.

Personally, I regretted that her choice had not fallen on the man she had asked down for Catherine's benefit. I had met his type abroad sometimes, the stuff of which ambassadors are made, suave, courteous, well-educated, well-groomed, a charming companion, a good *raconteur*. I recognised the name —Guy Bannister; he had done special correspondent work in '16 and '17, and had done it rather effectively, the Press declared. (Well, that only meant he was as good a liar as the next man, for Kipling was quite right about the nudity and consequent indecency of Truth.) Now I was told that he held office on some scientific review, and contributed articles to other people's. His, I reflected, scowling at Egerton, would be the kind of house where a man might care to stay. I didn't expect to see much of Rosemary after her marriage.

Presently I sat by Catherine and asked her if it were true and why.

"I believe so. He claims to be in love."

"Scarcely that," I suggested. "That sort of chap merely has preferences, and regulates his life accordingly."

"The odd thing is that Rosemary's infatuated. I hope it'll be all right. She's fluttered plenty of pulses in the past year or two."

"It'll take more than Rosemary to flutter this fellow's. A General Election, perhaps," for politics were stamped all over his face.

"All the same," Catherine added seriously, "he isn't quite all he looks. No, I'm not going to say anything more. Ask Simon sometime if you're curious. Personally, I shouldn't have been quite so ready to accept the position, but if he's satisfied I suppose it's all right. Simon's word is law with Rosemary, you know."

She left me with a sensation of something unfinished. Moreover, the name had struck some vague chord in my memory, but I could not place it. Nevertheless the thought persisted and left me disquieted.

IV

Nothing of any consequence happened during dinner. But we were all (except Bannister and Egerton, who were strangers and less aware of the tension) in a state of expectation, though none of us could have said what it was we feared.

After the women had gone upstairs Chandos seemed more than ever ill-at-ease. His hands (those beautiful hands!) toyed nervously with the stem of his wine-glass, which was empty, and with the cigar he did not light. Bannister broke the ice by discussing a book sale at Christie's, and Egerton, who appeared to be completely at home in five languages and six centuries of literature, took him up. Presently Chandos lost that absorbed look, and joined them, and I talked to Dacre. I saw with some surprise that the Sealyham terrier had slipped into dinner with him, and now sat on the chair Miss Dennis had vacated. Dacre must have felt entirely out of the drawing but for me, since art was a closed book to him, and his reading was confined to the *Field*, the *Sporting Times*, and Surtees' racing stories.

He told me about the litter of spaniels he was nursing down at Dacre Court. "Keen sale for them," he explained, "far more than for these chaps." He patted the dog affectionately. "Solomon," he added, with his wry, unhappy smile, "the friend that sticketh closer than a brother. He has his uses, like Captain Hook's crocodile, who swallowed the alarm-clock—you can always hear us coming and get away in time."

We did not stay downstairs long, and I think the women were glad of our presence. I was reminded suddenly of Barrie's, "Shall we join the Ladies?" The same eerie atmosphere prevailed here also.

Freyne is a wonderful place. Once it was an Abbey, and many of the guest-rooms are the one-time cells, though partitions have been taken down to enlarge the rooms. The corridors are flagged and uncarpeted in the upper part of the building, but downstairs great oak stairs have replaced the old stone ones that were worn—so says repute—into grooves where the monks' bare feet came slipping down noiselessly to keep their night watches in the chapel. This last was built for some reason on a kind of mezzanine floor, and was now carpeted and exquisitely papered and painted, and used as a drawing-room. The larger room, added by the Lord Freyne of the period a hundred and fifty years ago, is only thrown open on ceremonial occasions. In the second room, which we now entered, where the altar had once stood was a deep divan, along which Catherine lay like a moonbeam; on a wide monkish settle under the triptych window that shows St Cecilia with her lamb, St Lucy with a lily, and St Agnes carrying her breasts on a dish, Rosemary was waiting, her eager eyes fixed on the door.

The evening dragged on. That feeling of expectation increased and became quite horrible, until it was like a tangible element, choking and sickening us all. At last I discovered what it was—that queer, silent, menacing woman, Althea Dennis. Whatever sort of explosion was boding, she held the match. I thought of the poor devil in *The Pit and the Pendulum*, guarded by the never-sleeping eye. So was this woman watching, though she took no notice of us. It was Chandos whom she followed with her gaze as he moved round the room, not protectively, hungrily, tenderly, as he watched Catherine, but with a fierce impatience, as if she longed to rip him out of the trappings of Freyne and have him alone. I couldn't imagine what for. It did occur to me, though, as it had already done concerning Dacre, that these people of one idea are dangerous folk. Both of them had the fanatic's look; neither would stop at obstacles.

Even Catherine seemed touched by that unease. She began

to draw Chandos into her conversation, and the avidity with which he responded made every man present wince. Even young Egerton looked away. I liked him the better for that.

It is in the little things that tragedy lies. The evening had almost ended; the realisation that soon we should be free from the spell that overlaid us all, made us appear more natural. Even Althea Dennis' influence, dark though it was, lay like a fainter shadow about our security. And then, without warning, Tragedy came leaping into our midst. Chandos had turned towards his wife, and in so doing caught his foot in the fringes of an ancient Moorish rug and stumbled against her; involuntarily I saw his hand close about hers, and she, before she could control herself, flushed and recoiled with a sudden movement of horror, as though a beetle had run on to her arm. The next instant she recovered herself, crying "Simon, did you hurt yourself?" But it was too late. We had all seen and understood that gesture.

Rosemary saved a difficult situation by calling a swift question to Bannister, who took her up with the experience of his years. The rest of us followed their example, and the incident passed. But Chandos was quite silent. And when I turned my eyes away from his cruelly-hurt face I encountered the gaze of Althea Dennis, and shuddered before the remorseless cruelty and hate that smouldered there.

CHAPTER 2 THE MYSTERY OF THE LOCKED DOOR

I

That evening Chandos asked me to come down to his study and smoke and drink and hear him talk. He talked for a long time, beginning with Rupert Dacre. He asked me how I thought the man looked.

"Shockingly ill," I told him. "Never saw a fellow so changed. He was a kind of Mulvaney in France, a jolly, swaggering, debonair chap."

"Mulvaney had vultures tearing at his liver," Chandos reminded me sombrely. "The rescue party who dug that fellow out of the trench where a shell had buried him did him a bad turn. He'd be far happier underground, for there isn't a chance—not a chance—he'll ever get what he wants."

That seemed to me to prove that in his own way Chandos was as daft as the man he impugned.

"The War treated him extraordinarily badly," he went on, "not merely the game leg that invalided him out, but by leaving him as legacy a kind of shell-shock that made him terrified of the dark. Of course, he loathed himself for that fear (I learned of it by chance, coming on him when he was in the grip of the most ghastly terror I've ever witnessed), repressed it and it demanded interest at a hundred per cent. In a way he achieved what he set out for. Hardly a soul guessed that as soon as dusk came in the wheel of torture turned for him till daylight. He was haunted by dead men he'd known abroad. They used to come out of the shadows every night, stand over him—mutilated, dead, rotten. . . . It's amazing he isn't altogether demented. That's why he has that dog with him all the time. Dogs and cats, you know, axe peculiarly sensitive to spiritual phenomena. Dacre knew that and he won't stir without the beast. If by chance he shuts it into a room it howls till he lets it out. It's the only way he manages to preserve his sanity. Even now the darkness is a thing of horror to him; but if the dog is normal he knows it's just his imagination. If once the beast showed fright I believe he'd go mad, because he'd *know* the ghosts weren't just figments of a diseased brain. I suppose it's inevitable. All the same I wish he hadn't come down here."

"It can't be good for him to moulder at Dacre Court," I suggested.

"It isn't. But what's to be done? He lives there like a monk, with three ex-servicemen. That's the way his neurosis takes him."

"Why doesn't he go abroad, get a man's job? That would cure his neurosis."

"I sometimes think there isn't a cure," returned Chandos slowly, "except the one he can't have. But it's eating up his life like a cancer. He's lost to all sense of decency, gives himself away to the most casual stranger." He stopped sharply, and presently began to talk in a new voice. "Not that I've much right to speak of decency. If I had a spark of good feeling I suppose I'd release Catherine, let her be happy in her own way, and before God! Alan, I believe I would, if it were any other man. But she shan't go to that fellow. He's rotten all through; he won't stay the course. And that Catherine, whom I've set on a pedestal, should be one of a crowd of women in his gallery, is too much. What's one woman more or less to him? And I don't want to get hanged for murder, or see Catherine's picture on the front page of the *News of the World*. So there's no alternative really, and we shall both go on suffering like hell, till something happens. And that may not be far off."

I dared not speak of Catherine, but I did murmur something about his work, which was worth more than a dozen women, even such elusive, beautiful, maddening women as Catherine.

He shrugged the suggestion aside. "Work? But how much does that matter now? There was a time when all the women in the world couldn't have spoiled it—and they couldn't now. Only Catherine. She makes everything I do seem such a little thing, a drift of dust, something she could blow away with a single breath. And yet—it isn't as though I asked much of her, Alan. Just the barren pleasure of seeing her at my table at meal-times, of her company in walks and drives now and again. Men who aren't her husband get as much as that." He stopped again, and a spasm twisted his ugly, powerful face. But tonight, despite his exhaustion, it seemed fine, almost beautiful, and I thought with disgust of such tepid good looks as Egerton possessed.

"Another drink, Alan?" Chandos asked me in a stifled sort of voice. "Yes, you must join me. I can't talk any more tonight. I feel tired." As he spoke he took a little bottle of tablets from a cupboard in the wall. "Heart a trifle strained," he murmured apologetically. "Frobisher's given me these."

The sight I had of him, as he stood by the door and watched me mounting the stairs, turned all the sympathy I had felt for Catherine over to him. As I undressed I remembered his harsh words, and recalled also with a pang of dismay that I had never yet found him unjust in his estimate of a man. Moreover, there had been dare-devil stories in France.... A man with Dacre's face and temperament could no more avoid adventure than a moth could keep away from a light.

II

Catherine Chandos loved flowers; she knew what professors are only just beginning to find out, that they have hearts and pulses and are sensitive things. On my first morning at Freyne I woke late, and lay and watched the garden Catherine had made. It was a jolly, gay, old-fashioned affair, with tall, flaunting hollyhocks and foxgloves, and beds of candytuft and larkspur and a fiery bed of marigolds and borders of that little pink flower called London Pride. It was a still calm morning, full of peace and a sense of well-being. A wan mist hung over the Sussex Downs; presently it would dissolve into soft, sweeping clouds of rain, but now it made the sky look like a smoky pearl.

I was dressing, with the same sense of calm, forgetful for the moment of Chandos' tragedy when there came a hasty knock on the door, and Egerton broke in with more speed than is becoming before nine o'clock of a cloudy morning.

"What's up?" I asked him, for he was breathing quickly, as though he had been running.

He said stiffly, "Sorry to break in on you in this fashion, but you were with Chandos last night, weren't you? Did he say anything that led you to believe he might be contemplating sudden death?"

The shock of that silenced me. I tried to recall what Chandos had said last night. Suicide? It would cut the knot he declared he had not the courage to unloose in any other way. There had been that murmur, too, about the end being perhaps not very far off. But there I paused. Chandos was a gentleman, and there are disadvantages to such an estate. Even if he had plotted suicide he wouldn't have accomplished it at a time when he had his house filled with guests, including strangers, when Rosemary was about to announce her absurd engagement, particularly he would not take such a step after the incident of last night. The repetition of such a story, going the rounds of the county, would effectually blast Catherine's good name.

So I replied to young Egerton, who had just lighted a cigarette he forgot to smoke, and who was whiter than any fellow of his age has a right to be, "I'm certain he wasn't. What's happened?"

"I don't know," he returned coolly. "No one knows yet."

"Then, what the devil——?"

"Did he lock the door when you went away last night? No? Of course not. Why should he? The rest of the house was abed, and he couldn't reasonably expect to be disturbed. That was about twelve-thirty, wasn't it?"

"I'm afraid I didn't look at the clock," I said coldly, wondering if he suspected me of setting a knife in Chandos' throat.

"Half-past twelve," he repeated. "Bannister and I were talking on the balcony, and we heard you come up and I glanced at my watch."

"But, if nothing's happened. . . ."

"The door's locked now."

"Well?"

"That doesn't convey anything to you? A man (presumably) locks his door at twelve-thirty, when he should rather be thinking of bed, and at nine the next morning it's still locked, and he's on the other side of it?"

"He may have come out and locked it behind him."

"Then where is he now?"

"He may have gone out," I suggested feebly.

"With all the outer doors barred and bolted on the inside?"

"Perhaps he's still in there, asleep."

"Benson and two men and a bevy of women have been assaulting that door for some time. They've made enough row to wake the dead." That seemed to strike him as an unfortunate simile, for he frowned.

Another step sounded on the stairs. Another knock came at the door. Benson's voice said, "Sir!" and thoroughly alarmed now, I turned and went downstairs.

"I'm afraid, sir, we shall have to send for the locksmith," Benson explained, "It's a special lock Sir Simon had put on a year or two back."

"And has no one," asked Egerton languidly, "a duplicate key?"

"No, sir. Sir Simon wouldn't have one made. Pope here has been trying to open the door, but I think it's too much for him."

The chauffeur, who had been on his knees, fiddling with a piece of wire, rose apologetically. I sent him for the locksmith, and asked whether Catherine had been told.

"I think, sir, her maid, Peters, has told her. She sent a message that she would be down directly."

A new voice broke in on us, a voice so clotted with hatred that my blood ran cold. It was Althea Dennis, her face dark with a rush of blood, her hair wild; just so might Boadicea have looked when she headed a charge in her chariot with scythes on the wheels.

"Lady Chandos," she whispered, so low that I realised how violent was the storm of her passion, "what does she matter anyway? She killed him. I've seen this coming—and coming—for weeks. He's been waiting, waiting, for a single word from her, and she wouldn't say it. Hungry he's been—starved, half-mad—and she didn't care. I tell you," her voice rose, "she murdered him as surely as if she put a knife in his throat. He was a lonely man—all his life he was a lonely man—and she didn't care."

The servants had withdrawn to the passage behind the main staircase. I said roughly, "Why should you be so sure he's dead?" But Miss Dennis only laughed. Egerton put in woodenly, "Here is Lady Chandos," and Miss Dennis went quickly over to the narrow leaded windows giving on to the drive and the rather fine country road. Egerton also had the delicacy to remove himself out of earshot, so that I was left alone to greet Catherine. In the crude, unsympathetic light of nine o'clock she seemed like a ghost, the sad, unpeaceful ghost of their dead happiness. Agony was stamped on her white lips, on those bloodless cheeks; as for her eyes, I dared not look twice at the pain that turned them from gray to black. Even her voice was as dead as Chandos' departed hopes.

"Alan," whispered that dead voice, "she was right. If he is dead, then I've killed him. And yet I tried. . . ." She was silent a moment, thinking how she had tried, and how futile it had all been. Then, "I think, even in the grave, I shall be haunted by his face as I saw it last," she said.

"He may only have fainted," I suggested foolishly, "or perhaps he took a sleeping-draught," for I had just remembered the phial of tablets.

"Could any sleeping-draught keep him silent through all this?"

asked the ghost at my side. "Hammering and knocking. . . ." All the same, she went up to the door and turned the handle and beat on the panels with her palms, crying out his name and beseeching him to let her in. "Simon," she called, "Simon. It's I, your wife. You mustn't shut me out." It was all inexpressibly painful. Another minute and she would be raving with hysteria, and Chandos deserved such peace as he had achieved. But Miss Dennis stopped her with a brutality of which no man would be capable.

"What's the use of crying out to him *now*?" she demanded violently. "When he needed you, wanted you, prayed to you, you wouldn't come. Now it's too late. And even if it weren't, if he were to get up and open the door, you'd shrink again as you shrank last night. You're terribly sorry for yourself because you're hurt, and because you can't undo what you have done, and because it spoils your ease of mind. But you don't want him; you've never wanted him. Can't you let him be still, even in the grave?"

The white ghost stopped and turned. "You dare say such things to me?" muttered the pale lips.

"I have the right," said Althea Dennis, but before anything could be added there was a cry, and Rosemary came downstairs, with Bannister at her side, and Dacre limping just behind.

It seemed as though the locksmith would never come. We stood in a futile crowd in the hall. Bannister asked suddenly, "What about the window? Has any one tried?" and he moved expectantly. But Egerton, to whom Rosemary had instinctively turned, said unemotionally, "Shuttered; locked on the inside. Impossible. Benson and I have tested them."

We fell silent after that till the locksmith appeared. Even then it was a long job. I saw, without realising it, a score of paltry details. That Catherine, sunk on an old chest by the door, had clasped her hands tightly in her lap, to prevent herself from complete breakdown; that Bannister was murmuring something that did not seem to console her at all; that Egerton's hands, thrust casually into his pockets, were clenched into fists; that now, when it didn't matter, we were all careful to be particularly quiet. We spoke only in whispers, and when some one stumbled over Solomon and he whined, Catherine said urgently, "Take him up, Rupert," as though even that noise might disturb the man behind the locked door. But Solomon barked so loudly (as was his wont when lifted), that Dacre set him down again, and the last spark of hope died out of our hearts, for that noise would have aroused any but a dead man.

Then the locksmith rose at last, saying, "Job's done, me lady," and melted unobtrusively into the crowd of servants who clustered in the background, anxious to solve the mystery.

Catherine looked piteously to me. "Come with me, Alan," she whispered, so we went in together, and Rosemary and Egerton and Althea Dennis followed us. Dacre, I noted, paused by the door, his hand twisted in his dog's collar, as though he feared it might bark again, and with him stayed Bannister, who was almost a stranger, and, like me, wished himself anywhere else.

Chandos was sitting by the table, bent over it as though the business of living had been too much for him at last. In his hand was a pen and before him was a sheet half-filled with his zigzag writing, and on the table and the floor and all round him were other papers, carelessly crumpled and tossed aside. But my eyes were all for the small bottle I had seen the night before and that still stood by him. Nine hours ago it had been three-parts full, whereas now it was half-empty. So this was the answer to Simon Chandos' sleeplessness, his haggard air, his wild unrest. Morphine!

Catherine seemed to have lost her fear, for she came over to him, put her arms about him, bent down to look into his eyes. It didn't matter; nothing could either exalt or embitter him now. He was quite dead, had been dead for some time, and it seemed that the whole room was empty and lifeless and cold, because hitherto it had drawn all its vitality from him, who had left it for ever.

Catherine stood up at last, stiff and straight and tall; her eyes were no longer dark, but hard like glass, because something in her had been frozen.

"Was it all my fault?" she whispered, but no one spoke. There wasn't anything to say. "And how . . .?" she went on, and then, seeing the bottle, she touched it. "Morphine? Isn't that a drug?"

We told her that it was.

"I didn't know. Of course, artists do sometimes; they live on their nerves, don't they? But it's rather—awful."

Althea Dennis, with scant regard for decency, broke into the group. She was too glad of her power to be pitiful. "He took morphine because he was dying of cancer," she said deliberately. "He suffered so."

"Why didn't I know that?" cried Catherine, beginning to live again.

"Perhaps he was afraid of seeing you flinch from him. But no, it wasn't that, of course. He couldn't have thought such a thing of you. He didn't tell you because he was afraid of hurting you. He didn't want you to be troubled for him. But he had to tell some one, so he told me. "Me," and she struck her breast like a stage heroine. "You thought of me as nothing but a machine to serve him; yes, and I was glad to be that. When he came back, blue and worn-out, he hid himself from you. He never thought to hide himself from me. I didn't count, you see. I wasn't human —to him. And yet," her voice became fierce and passionate, "it's I, not you, who would have given him everything I had if he'd wanted it, just for a day, for an hour, to soothe him. I loved him as your kind of woman doesn't understand love. I didn't want anything from him, just wanted to be allowed to wait on him, to be a mat under his feet. He never guessed. But all I could do was to take a little bit of his pain, I who would have borne it all and thanked Heaven for the chance. I saw him suffer as you didn't know he could suffer. But he's at peace now; you can't hurt him any more. Presently you'll be happy again; there'll be another man for you. It's not like that for me. I begin to die today; but I shall die richer than you've ever lived."

I suppose it was inexcusable melodrama, but it cowed us all, we were quite silent, quite awed by the tremendous majesty of an undesired woman's passion for poor, splendid, deformed Simon Chandos. When that moment of awe and silence had passed I realised something else, which was the reason why he had practically flung me out of the room last night, because another of those terrible attacks of pain was upon him, and I was his guest.

Miss Dennis turned to me suddenly. "Did he say nothing to you?"

I told her "Nothing," and I saw a strange, dark happiness in her eyes at this proof that she alone had been in his confidence. Then Rosemary, disengaging herself from Egerton's restraining hand, came closer to me, and said, "He died writing something, Alan. Perhaps it's a letter."

I glanced at Catherine, who replied, in that thin shrill voice, "Will some one read it aloud? We're all concerned, and we'd better all hear. No, not Miss Dennis." Miss Dennis laughed; she was the sort of woman who could laugh even in the presence of death. "I don't want to hear it, even," she exclaimed contemptuously, "it's nothing to do with me." But neither Dacre nor Bannister made any attempt to move from the door, so she stayed after all. I fancy she intended to, anyway. Egerton, who had regained his normal composure—after all, what did the death of Simon Chandos mean to him?—asked calmly, "Shall I read it, Lady Chandos?" and, stepping up to the body, he read over the dead man's shoulder.

It was an incoherent, almost indecipherable screed, and Egerton read it very slowly, which was why the words, with pauses between each, seemed like a judgment delivered against us:—

"Forgive me for taking this way. It is the only path to freedom we may take with dignity and honour. You will think that if I loved you more finely I could let you go where you would find happiness; but though I could bear to lose you dead, I could not lose you living. It is for love of you that I choose this road. For the joy and beauty you gave me I shall always be grateful: it will make even the grave warm and sweet."

And then, almost at the foot of the page, he had written the words of Sidney Carton on the scaffold:

"It is a far, far better thing that I do than I have ever done; it is a far, far better rest that I go to . . ."

"That's all," said Egerton, stepping back again. "He doesn't finish the quotation."

Bannister spoke from the silence by the door. "He quoted that last night. And now it's his epitaph." Then he flushed uncomfortably, for he was only a stranger, and the dead man's wife stood near by.

By this time there had begun to spread among us all a feeling of intrusion, because we were disturbing the peace that Chandos had deliberately created for himself, the only peace he had known for many weeks. Rosemary, who had loved him, voiced our general opinion by saying urgently, "Come away now; we can't do anything, and he doesn't want us."

"No," agreed Catherine in a queer low voice, "of course he doesn't. I suppose I must telephone Dr Frobisher, though he can't do anything either."

Dacre and Bannister went out quickly, but when I turned to shut the door I found Egerton still by the body.

"Come on!" I bade him curtly.

"There's something here that puzzles me," he returned without moving. "I've only just noticed it."

It was his voice rather than the words that brought us back, apprehensive and startled, into the room.

"What do you mean?"

"He's holding his pen in the right hand."

"Well, how do men usually hold their pens?" Then I stopped, remembering what had already occurred to him, that Chandos was a left-handed man. He habitually wrote and painted with his left hand, and it was barely conceivable that in his hour of agony he would leave a dying message written with the hand he never used.

Once again it was Rosemary who spoke first. "Alan, what does it mean? Scott!" She turned swiftly from one to other of us.

Egerton repeated dispassionately, "He was a left-handed man."

We tried, panic-stricken, to find some explanation, said he might have laid the pen aside and have been playing with it idly: and more to the same effect, all except Egerton, who said nothing. Presently we, too, fell silent. The fact was indisputable. There was Chandos sitting at his table, and in his right hand a pen whose nib still rested where the next word should come. Besides, men fidgeting idly don't hold things in that purposeful grip.

Dacre, who accepted new ideas slowly, said in a heavy voice, "Then, if he couldn't have put it there himself, some one did it for him—foul play."

No one answered him, but after a minute Rosemary exclaimed, "The key! The door was locked. How could any one get in?"

"How," asked Egerton woodenly, "could any one get out?"

"How?" we chorused.

"Why not through the door? The key isn't in it. In fact, we haven't yet found a key."

"When a man locks himself into a room," said Dacre, "he puts the key on the table, or in his pocket."

"Look, Alan," murmured Catherine, so I put my hand into the right pocket.

"Not there," Egerton warned me dryly, "a man who can't use his right hand doesn't use his right pocket either."

His confounded logic was justified, of course. I found the key in the other pocket and laid it on the table.

Catherine went on, still in that low, tense voice, "Then how did—any one get in?" She shrank, like the rest of us, from the word "murderer," for it has an ugly sound, and we and the servants were the only people in the house.

We talked a little, desultorily, trying to find some answer to the puzzle, all except Egerton, who was very silent again; but of course we could arrive at no conclusion whatsoever, so at last we left poor Chandos alone and went into the hall. Only at the door Egerton turned and muttered something I could not catch.

"What was it?" I asked Rosemary, but she said she hadn't heard either, only that it was something about not looking upon his like again. I wished more than ever that Chandos had lived long enough to tell me the story Catherine wouldn't repeat; and as though she read my thoughts, Rosemary put in earnestly, "You think, Alan, that he's a machine; you'll find you're wrong. When he cares for any one it isn't for a day."

I looked over my shoulder: Egerton was standing alone near the window Miss Dennis had chosen that morning, and a shaft of pale sunlight fell full on his face. When I saw him I knew that Rosemary had a deeper insight than I had hitherto imagined.

III

While we waited for Frobisher we went into the dining-room and pretended to eat breakfast. As I drank coffee and tried to persuade Rosemary to do the same I had an uncanny feeling that at any moment the door would open and Chandos would come in, looking for us, because Eternity was so lonely. Though probably it couldn't be lonelier than his life had been.

Frobisher came soon afterwards, in an indifferent temper and in great haste, because there was a child in the Cottage Hospital with a gangrened appendix, awaiting operation.

"Can't stop more than a minute," he rapped out. He was a gaunt, lofty chap, with a white beard and white hair. "Where is he?"

It came to me with an odd sense of shock that already a sick village child was of more importance than Simon Chandos.

The library was untouched; even the glasses we had used the night before and the stumps of the cigars we had smoked lay on the table. Frobisher stooped—he had to stoop a long way—and looked into the dead man's eyes.

"Eyeballs very contracted," he said shortly. "Morphine poisoning? Possibly. There'll have to be a post-mortem, of course. But why . . .?" He caught sight of the phial and picked it up. "You may be right, then. When did he have these?"

"I couldn't tell you." Catherine's wan voice floated out to us, as tremulous and insubstantial as thistledown. "I never knew he did have them."

"Didn't know he was dying by inches of cancer, I suppose? Wouldn't tell you, of course. Damned fool. Just like him, though. The biggest fool and the finest gentleman I ever met."

Remembering Egerton, I looked across to him of a sudden and I saw an odd light pass over his face, as though he endorsed the doctor's words. "Sent him to Strickland three months ago," Frobisher continued, "though I hadn't any doubts. Strickland agreed. Liver a cancerous mass. Suffered like the devil, though I suppose he never let on. Where's that woman—what's her name?—who keeps his papers?"

Miss Dennis came in, and said that Chandos had had the tablets on such and such a date. She turned up a file and showed a receipt for them.

"No right to have taken all these," scowled Frobisher. "Did you see the bottle yesterday or the day before?"

"I haven't seen it since it arrived," she returned sulkily. "Sir Simon kept it locked in a cupboard, because he never knew when the pain would come on. But he sent me away first—always."

"Did no one see it last night? It is very important to establish some kind of a clue."

Catherine said in her exhausted voice, "Mr Ravenswood was with him till half-past twelve."

He turned in a flash. "Ravenswood! Didn't know you were here. About these tablets. . . ."

"I saw Chandos take them out of the cupboard last night. He took two—I remember seeing them lie for an instant on the table as he put the cork back—and told me that his heart was a trifle strained, and he was taking these under your direction. I didn't think much about it. So many men have some patent pill."

"Exactly. But this wasn't a patent pill. It was a dangerous drug. I'd have staked my life Chandos was a safe man." He scowled and pulled his beard; he was a man who hated to find trust misplaced.

"He was a safe man," I reassured him, and he swung round angrily. "What the devil d'ye mean by that?"

I glanced across at Catherine, who was as white as death. Her appealing eyes met mine.

"I mean this," I told him bluntly. "Chandos, as you know, was a left-handed man, but when we found him this morning he was holding a pen tightly in the right hand."

Frobisher, oblivious to Catherine, rapped out a wicked word, and turning in a flash, stooped and examined the hands. Very carefully he removed the pen and strove to straighten the finger.

"As I thought," he told me, replacing the pen, "the muscles have stiffened. More a detective's job than mine, though no man in his senses will believe that a normally left-handed man uses his right hand in the last moments of his life. Besides, this is his usual handwriting. The thing can't be done. He told me once that he never used the right hand. Try and write with your left hands, you right-handed men, and see what's the result. Another point. Look at the position of the pen. No man curls his index finger round a pen like that. And, as it happens, Chandos damaged that finger two years ago, and it's left it stiff, so he wouldn't have attempted to use it. It's been twisted deliberately into position to give the impression of a man writing and suddenly interrupted. Whoever did it didn't imagine that in the shock and horror any one would notice such minute details. Perhaps he didn't even know about the hands. Probably no one knew about the finger. Chandos wasn't the sort of chap to talk about himself."

With characteristic coolness he leaned forward and read the letter. "'It is a far, far better rest that I go to than I have ever known.' Has it ever occurred to you, Ravenswood, what a lonely thing is the human soul? Wanders about in a small enclosure of its own, and blunders against riddles it can't read, and tries to find some common tongue with which to communicate with the world—or God—and at last goes back into the darkness." And then he, too, was silent. He took no further notice of Catherine. For, as Dacre was blind to the beauty of Art, so was Frobisher blind to the beauty of women, except as child-bearers. A married woman who had not fulfilled her normal function was to him so much lumber, a machine that is out of order and should be scrapped. Women called him a hard man.

He spoke again abruptly. "Then your suggestion is that after you'd gone he took more tablets—many more—to allay the hellish pain? Two would be a stiff dose, but even if he were enduring the tortures of the damned he wouldn't take a dozen at a gulp. The thing's incredible."

Then he remembered the child with the gangrened appendix, and pulled on his gloves, saying that there was enough death in the world as it was. But his voice was angry, for he disliked being foiled.

"But when . . .?" Catherine began, and he turned and touched the dead man professionally.

"He's been dead about two hours. Who was the last to see him?"

"I was," I repeated. "Twelve-thirty."

"Ten hours ago. This stuff, injected, takes normally six to twelve hours to kill a man. But taken through the mouth it requires much more time to become effective. It must have been taken almost immediately you left him. Even so I don't understand it. I shall have to wait till I've had time to examine the body. I've known one grain prove fatal, and recovery after thirty-five. He was accustomed to taking two at a time, was he? And they're quarter-grain tablets. Well, it's on the cards he took a grain on his own account. But that doesn't explain the missing tablets. I must wait for the post-mortem."

He turned back to Catherine at last. "You'd better get a man up from the station. This ought to be reported at once. Or perhaps, Ravenswood, you can do it instead of Lady Chandos. I'll be back before lunch to examine the body thoroughly, though I doubt if we can learn much until an autopsy has been made."

He went off, a Triton among minnows, in his muddy, shabby little car, and Catherine and I were left facing one another. At last she spoke. "But the key, Alan! The key that was in his pocket! If he was poisoned, how did the murderer get away?" She began to shiver, and blue lines showed under her eyes, and she put one hand on my arm and said, "Suppose—suppose he's hidden there still?"

"Of course he isn't," I reassured her, wondering what on earth I was going to do if she collapsed into hysterics. "I'll ring up the station and look after this chap when he comes. You go and lie down. There's nothing you can do."

She drew a little away from me, and stood there very stiff and straight and cold. "No," she repeated after me, "there's nothing. Of all the things Simon wanted me to do for him I never did one. How that doctor despises me, but nothing compared with how much I despise myself."

CHAPTER 3 THE STEP IN THE NIGHT

I

The police station sent us, almost immediately, a fellow called Bradlaugh who had come to Freyne on the track of a jobbing gardener, who was a forger in his spare time. Having gated him, Bradlaugh was about to return to the Yard when the murder of Simon Chandos put another job in his way. He was a sharp-featured, middle-aged man, with a narrow head and a chin so long that his mouth came in the middle of his face.

Catherine came down to meet him, but just as she was leading the way to the library, where the body still lay, there was a sound behind her and Althea Dennis exclaimed, "One moment, Lady Chandos. There's something to be said first. And I must say it now when you're all here and before the detective has said a word, so that no one may suggest later that I thought of the story to fit in with the evidence." Her bitter eyes challenged and scorned us all, "No one has been asked yet about what happened in the night, but I was lying awake a little after one, and I distinctly heard a step on the stairs. It went past my door like some one trying to be very quiet, but I heard it all the same. I sleep very lightly, and I was puzzled that Sir Simon had not come to bed."

"Was there anything particularly strange about his sitting up?"

"He doesn't do it usually."

"Or any special reason why you should be listening for him last night?"

Miss Dennis flushed a curious mottled shade. "I couldn't bear to think of him all alone there all night. I knew he was miserable."

"And you knew beyond question that he had not come up?"

She dropped her eyes. "I'd know his step among a million," she said, with a kind of passionate sullenness.

"And you heard a step about half-past one?"

"About one. It came down the stairs and went past my door."

"A man's step?"

"Yes."

"Did you recognise it?"

"It was the step of a man who is lame."

"Have you any suspicions?"

"There's only one man here whom the cap fits. That's Captain Dacre."

Dacre had been listening with an appearance of interest that was interest only so far as Catherine was concerned, but he changed colour at that, blanching like a girl. His eyes turned instinctively to Catherine, as if he expected her somehow to save him from suspicion. And she did, though not in the manner any of us anticipated. She seemed calm enough as she turned to us all and began to speak, but her eyes were too bright and she wrung her hands together so that we shouldn't see them tremble. When she spoke it was to Miss Dennis.

"Did you hear the step go down again?"

Miss Dennis looked sulky, "No, I didn't. But then I'm almost the whole length of the corridor away from the staircase."

Catherine shook her head slightly. "You didn't hear it," she said slowly, "because it didn't go down—any farther."

There was a moment's silence while we realised what she meant. Then Rosemary broke out, sick and incredulous, "Catherine—you can't mean...."

Catherine made a convulsive gesture. "Be quiet, Rosemary. How should you understand?"

She stood looking from face to face, gathering like wine into a chalice what she read in each. From me, outrage that she should have taken that high risk and put a loyal man to open shame; from Rosemary, only horror; from Egerton, disgust; from Althea Dennis, a white-hot anger that any woman should dare hold Simon Chandos so cheap. Only from Bannister, who had lived long enough to learn compassion for the wildness of love and the frailty of humanity did she gather sympathy. Bradlaugh was untouched, but then he had the soul of a Robot, and had heard such tales before.

He said expressionlessly, "Am I to understand. Lady Chandos, that you can prove an alibi for Captain Dacre at such a time?"

Catherine said simply, "Yes. He was with me."

Our amazement at such a story was the greater, since, both before and since her marriage, Catherine had shunned even the fringe of that Society that assuages its boredom with lovers and suchlike. Dacre seemed struck dumb by her courage; he watched her with the look of a man terribly hurt, yet exalted by the source of his pain. For the moment he was absolutely silent. He could hardly have expected her to prove her love so publicly. But when he heard her give that reply, he blundered on to the scene, as always, a gate behind the rest of the hunt.

"No," he said harshly, "that isn't true. Lady Chandos says that to shield me...."

As Noah's dove dipped and flew for the olive-spray, so did Bradlaugh clutch at that indiscretion.

"Shield you from what?"

"Suspicion."

"Of murder?"

Dacre looked distrait. "I suppose so."

"Why should you be suspect?"

"From one point of view, the unexpected death of Sir Simon might be reckoned as highly advantageous—from a legal point of view, probably your own. In actual fact, it makes little difference. Or rather, the difference is my loss."

"If you would cease speaking in riddles," said Bradlaugh

sharply.

"I don't propose to discuss my private affairs," answered Dacre, groping for a dignity he had long since forfeited. "But Lady Chandos knew of this matter, and realising that that, taken with Miss Dennis' evidence, would make the picture black for me, she invented on the spur of the moment her gallant story. I never moved out of my room all night. I went up to bed early with a splitting head, and didn't wake till one of the servants roused me."

"You ask us to believe that none of the din going on downstairs wakened you?"

"I invariably sleep deeply; very deeply." But as he spoke, he changed colour again, and fidgeted, like a man who has something to hide.

Bradlaugh turned back to Miss Dennis. "You're sure you only heard one step?"

"Only one; a dragging, furtive step going stealthily past, and but for that not a sound in the whole silent house."

"You did not look out?"

"It didn't occur to me to suspect any of the guests of murder."

"And this morning?"

"When the servants told me the door was locked I thought that perhaps the pain had been too awful, and Sir Simon had taken a double dose of the tablets, and was asleep. A double dose wouldn't kill him."

"You were entirely in his confidence regarding the drug?"

She seemed troubled. "I knew he had it."

"Did any one else know? This is most important."

"I don't think so. He cared particularly that Lady Chandos should not know."

"For his own sake, or hers?"

"Hers, of course. He'd have been tortured on the wheel to save her a moment's pain. And she'd have let him lie there to give herself an instant's joy."

Bradlaugh let that go. Through all Catherine's agony, through Dacre's anger and fierce denials, through Miss Dennis' bitter hostility, I never saw him anything but composed.

"What is the strength of the tablets?"

"A quarter of a grain. He took two at a time."

"Ah! I think for the moment that is all. Later..."

But she interrupted him savagely. "No, not quite. Captain Dacre has refused to give you his reason for wishing Sir Simon out of the way, but I can tell you. Sir Simon had advanced him ten thousand pounds on the security of Dacre Court, to be repaid within seven years. The time is up next week. Ask Captain Dacre if he has the money ready."

Bradlaugh scarcely bothered to turn his head. We all knew Dacre wasn't in a position to return such a sum. But that news made me more apprehensive than if they had found definite traces of the man's presence in the library. For Dacre Court was part of his heritage and his tradition. He loved this house of his as other men love women; add to that his devastating passion for the dead man's wife, and the case against him was black enough to justify all Catherine's fears.

Dacre spoke harshly, addressing us all. "Of course I can't repay it. Chandos knew it. But he didn't propose to take advantage of that."

"You're certain?"

"Absolutely. He wrote to say so."

"You have the letter?"

Dacre became suddenly restive, muttering something about letters being private, and not keeping them.

"If you could produce it," Bradlaugh insinuated. But Dacre shook his head. "Afraid you'll have to take my word for it." But at that stage his word wasn't likely to help him much.

"And you still deny absolutely that you left your room in the night for any reason whatsoever?"

"Certainly I deny it absolutely. As for Lady Chandos' story, it was a piece of divine charity."

But Bradlaugh was a CID man, and had no use for divine charity. He wanted facts. He had nothing more at the moment to say to Dacre, so he turned to Catherine, saying in a voice of dismissal, "Lady Chandos, I should like Sir Simon's lawyer to be summoned. Meanwhile, I propose to seal all the rooms. I note you have a telephone here in the hall. There will be no need, therefore, to use any of the extensions."

When he had done that he came back to us asking who was the last to see Chandos alive.

Egerton answered in his soft, dry voice, "The murderer, presumably."

"The two," returned the detective, eyeing him steadily, "are sometimes synonymous."

II

I was the first to undergo examination. The questions at the outset followed the road Frobisher had already raked, and brought the same replies, until Bradlaugh said, "There's one other point that is bound to be offensive to you, and equally bound to be raised. I understand you were an intimate friend of the dead man. You were with him within a very short time of his death. Did he say anything that made you think he was even faintly considering suicide?"

"I certainly gained no such impression, and I find it impossible to believe that he would have chosen such a time."

"Did he say anything of altered plans?"

I answered him in Chandos' own words.

"That the end might not be far off," Bradlaugh repeated. "What did you understand by that?"

"At the moment, nothing. Now it seems likely that he was thinking of the few months left him."

"Possibly. Now, to come to the crux of the situation. Did he speak of Lady Chandos? I gather that their relations were purely formal."

"I can hardly be expected to discuss that," I said warmly. Bradlaugh sighed. His manner was very patient, as he explained that unless I told him what he wanted to know he would have to turn to Althea Dennis. "I should be sorry to be forced to do that," he added, "she doesn't strike me as an entirely impartial witness."

"For Heaven's sake don't listen to anything she'll tell you," I besought him hastily. She was so convulsed with passion that at that moment she would gladly have sworn Catherine's life away.

So Bradlaugh won, after all, and I told him what I knew, which wasn't very much.

"Had Sir Simon any suspicion of intimate relations between his wife and Captain Dacre?"

"He never spoke of such a thing to me."

"Nor hinted at the possibility?"

"He said Captain Dacre's position was hopeless."

"Why should he think that?"

"I don't know. I imagined he meant that whatever happened he didn't propose abdicating in Captain Dacre's favour."

"Did he say anything else about Captain Dacre?"

I hesitated. No one wants to damn a poor devil who is already blackened by the smokes of hell. All the same, if he had had a hand in murdering Chandos, hanging was too good for him. So I said at last, "Sir Simon did not, I'm certain, suspect disloyalty either from his wife or his friend. He knew he'd only got a year and probably thought it best to let matters settle themselves."

"Quite. It was unfortunate for them that they had not the advantage of that knowledge. If Sir Simon had told you that he had no intention of freeing Lady Chandos, obviously the only thing that could liberate her would be his death. Now, when you left the library last night, did Sir Simon lock the door?"

"I didn't hear him. But he was in the grip of a bad bout of pain, and he may have turned the key, fearing to be disturbed."

Bradlaugh frowned. "The more obvious explanation is that he didn't lock the door, that he was surprised by the murderer, who locked it, accomplished his job, left the key in Sir Simon's pocket, and escaped by another exit."

I asked him mildly how one forcibly fed a man with morphine tablets, whereat he scowled more blackly still. "I understand the examination of the body has not yet been made? What proof have you that the morphia was actually taken through the mouth? It is more than likely that Sir Simon, already drowsy with the morphia he had himself swallowed, was taken off his guard, and the drug injected subcutaneously. Then unconsciousness would supervene in a brief period. The murderer, safe behind the locked door, could then set the stage, and get back to his room without being observed. It is vastly improbable that any one will suspect murder; the tablets are on the table. The morphia found in the body will correspond with the number of tablets missing—roughly, that is. These tablets contain a quarter of a grain apiece. Presumably Sir Simon would take two. It has not yet been found how much morphia there is in the stomach, but two to three grains might well kill a man in Sir Simon's health. The murderer extracts, say a dozen tablets —you have yourself given evidence that there were many more in the bottle when you saw it at midnight than there are now— disposes of them, leaves a clear impression of suicide and waits for the inevitable discovery."

"Why should you be so sure?" I muttered, only half-convinced.

"The doctor—what did you say his name was?—Frobisher—will bear me out that it's practically impossible for a man to take a dozen tablets at a gulp, and in any case it's highly improbable that he would be dead within seven hours. Besides, no murderer would attempt to poison a man with morphine in tabloid form."

"And the missing tablets?"

"Are one half of the missing evidence."

"And the other?"

"The syringe that was used. I want to wait for the doctor's return before I touch the body, but I'm certain already in my own mind."

"So that's why you've sealed the rooms?"

"Exactly. And even then I was called several hours too late."

"And the key?"

"A secret exit, I should say. The house is old enough. I shall be able to tell you more when I've searched the room."

I told him that I had never heard of such a thing, but he

dismissed such scepticism, his lifted shoulders saying that it was easier to believe in a secret passage than in a murderer who could pass through a locked door.

After that he examined the servant who had found the door fastened. The girl said she had tried to open it, but it had not yielded; she had then rattled the handle without effect, and peered through the keyhole to know if the key were still in the lock. Afterwards she had knocked several times on the door.

"Why?" asked Bradlaugh unsympathetically. "What did you expect to happen?"

"I—I don't rightly know, sir. But I was frightened."

"What of?"

"Well, sir, it seemed odd that it should be locked, and no key be anywhere, but presently I thought perhaps he'd left some important papers there as he didn't want disturbed. Then when Mr Masters, him as is valet to Sir Simon, come down and says the master hasn't been to bed all night, we got scared, and Mr Benson come and have a look at it, and he said he was afraid something must have happened."

"You say that previously you had thought it was all right?"

The girl looked nervous, "Well, sir, how was I to know?"

"Didn't the light warn you that something was wrong?"

"Light, sir?"

"Yes, the electric light in the library. If you looked through the keyhole, or under the crack of the door you couldn't help seeing it."

She stared at him blankly. "There wasn't no light on."

"Quite sure?"

"Yes, sir. All the others'll say the same as me."

"I'll see," observed Bradlaugh grimly, sending for all the servants who had been present at the opening of the door, and examining them in turn. He got the same answer from them all. The room had been unlighted when the door was forced.

"And you?" asked Bradlaugh, turning to me suddenly.

"I'll swear it wasn't on."

He nodded. "That fact alone should be almost enough proof

that it wasn't suicide."

"I don't quite follow you," I confessed.

"Don't you see that if a man's committing suicide he'll sit at his table till the drug overpowers him? It won't occur to him to switch off the light, and then grope his way in the darkness back to his chair. I see that there is no desk lamp in Sir Simon's room, but that all the bulbs are controlled by the switch by the door. On the other hand, if he had been murdered, the criminal's first instinct would be to snap off all lights in case of discovery."

His logic was indisputable.

Then it was Egerton's turn. He was perfectly cool and at ease.

"You were up very early?" Bradlaugh suggested.

"It would scarcely be reckoned early by my colleagues in London."

"Still, earlier than the house was ready?"

"I suppose so, since no one was down. But I'm accustomed to early rising. My political work often begins at four in the morning."

"Still," Bradlaugh pressed, "earlier than is usual in country houses?"

"I can't say. I so rarely stay in them."

"Had you heard anything of the assault on the library door before you came down?"

"Sir Simon told us at dinner last night that Freyne is so constructed that the upper floors are practically sound-proof. I heard nothing that aroused my suspicions."

"Why should you choose Mr Ravenswood rather than—say, Captain Dacre—when you realised there was something amiss?"

"He was Sir Simon's most intimate friend, and was with him until a short time before his death."

"What," asked Bradlaugh sharply, "are we to understand by that?"

"I heard him come upstairs at half-past twelve. I happened to glance at my watch as the step went past my door. No, it isn't a habit of mine to look at my watch every time I hear a footstep, but under Providence I did so last night, and so can prove Mr

Ravenswood's alibi."

"And you were the first to notice the pen in the right hand?"

"I believe so. That's nothing very strange. I am trained to observation."

Bradlaugh got nothing out of him, and he retired shortly afterwards, as unruffled as when he appeared. The detective and I exchanged covert glances. Both of us realised that he knew more than he cared to tell.

Catherine took his place. She held her head high with the courage of a woman who had tossed her reputation over the windmill and refused to be crushed on that account. But it was a pitiful, defiant affair. To her proud nature it must have been a vile degradation to submit to the questions of a man without any particular sensitiveness or delicacy. She repeated her story of Dacre coming to her at a quarter to one, by which time she believed the rest of the house to be abed.

"Including Sir Simon?"

"I did not know."

"You heard Mr Ravenswood come up?"

"I heard a step at half-past twelve."

"You did not think that might be your husband?"

"I should know his step."

"You are certain it was half-past twelve? Not later?"

"No, not later."

"How can you be so sure?"

She hesitated. Then she whispered in a tone so low that it was scarcely audible, "I was watching the clock."

She did not add, because there was no need, that that was to be sure her lover would run no risk of detection. In any case, she was paying heavily for that hour of madness.

"How long did Captain Dacre remain with you?"

"Till a little after five." For all her courage it was becoming obvious that she was wilting. Already she drooped like a flower on its stem. But Bradlaugh's profession didn't allow him to be spendthrift of pity and he went on undeterred. Presently he wrung from her an admission that she had watched the time so closely because she was afraid of some servant going to Dacre's room and finding it empty. The clock, she told him, was a blue folding one standing by the bedside. After that he did let her go, but she was broken now, beautiful still, but broken....

Dacre had nothing new to add. He still refused to produce the letter from Chandos; otherwise he stuck to his absurd story. Divine charity he had called it; it seemed a pity he couldn't accept it as such.

Once again Althea Dennis was able to confuse him. She knew, at any rate, much that that letter had contained, though, she said, Chandos had written it in his own hand. It had been to ask Dacre not to come down to Freyne! So perhaps he had had his suspicions, after all.

"You have, of course, no copy of the letter?" Bradlaugh suggested.

"I haven't. I could tell you when it was posted, if that would help." She looked up a big book, bound in imitation grain leather, and said, "July 17th."

"Did Sir Simon discuss the matter with you at all?"

"He merely told me that he had suggested that Captain Dacre would save himself unnecessary pain if he refused the invitation."

"Meaning, presumably, Captain Dacre's feeling towards Lady Chandos?"

"And the fact that he would never be able to marry her."

"Why should you say that?"

"It's what he said."

"That he could never marry her? Or never would? The distinction is important."

"He said, 'He will never marry her.'"

"Did you gather from that that he meant to take forcible steps to prevent such a marriage?"

Miss Dennis stared. "As long as he was alive they couldn't marry."

"But after his death?"

"How could he stop them?"

"He might have added some clause to his will depriving Lady Chandos of her inheritance if she married Captain Dacre."

"I haven't seen the will," returned Miss Dennis sullenly, "and as far as injuring Captain Dacre is concerned, Sir Simon liked him in a way."

"In a way?"

"Well, he was sorry for him. He'd helped him often and often —he had no luck with money, and if it hadn't been for Sir Simon he'd have gone under long ago."

"Then presumably his meaning was that so long as he was alive Captain Dacre's position was hopeless?"

"I suppose so."

"But he knew he had to die within the year," cried Bradlaugh triumphantly.

"I don't know," said Miss Dennis flatly. "I'm simply repeating to you what he said."

"Thank you. And in spite of that letter Captain Dacre did come down to Freyne?"

"He said there were some important details he wished to discuss with Sir Simon, affecting the future."

"Sir Simon suspected nothing."

"No. He trusted the men he thought were his friends."

"Was there any disagreement between them?"

"Nothing outwardly."

"Sir Simon never spoke of such a thing?"

She answered with a faint hint of bitterness. "If he had it wouldn't have been to me."

"So that when Captain Dacre spoke of plans for the future he did not mean anything connected with Lady Chandos' future also?"

"I don't know." Her voice became suddenly strident. "Of course, it was just a cloak—a cloak for this vile intrigue. . . ." Bradlaugh silenced her instantly. I admired that man. Then he asked her for a plan of the house.

III

Freyne has been rebuilt and patched and restored so often since the early Norman work made the county beautiful that it is now a comparatively small place. The Puritans demolished much of it, and for a good many years it was left to the mercy of storm and raiders, until the Lord Freyne of the period dared come back from France, whither alien winds had driven him, and take up his inheritance under the Hollandish prince. It has an irregular and shapeless appearance, for succeeding generations have added to or altered the original structure.

On the whole there is more room inside than one might imagine from the exterior. On the ground floor were the billiard-room, the dining-hall, that was once a refectory, the morning-room and the library. On the next floor, a kind of mezzanine landing, were the huge drawing-room, (that was seldom used) the old chapel, where coffee was taken and bridge was played night after night, and a kind of boudoir where Catherine wrote her letters and interviewed prospective servants. At the end of a short corridor that spoilt all the symmetry of the floor was a small room where Althea Dennis had her typewriter, and where she might sit when her work was done. On the first floor proper was Catherine's suite of rooms, together with quarters for her maid. On the other side of the wide landing, up three polished stairs, were Chandos' apartments. Between the two were a couple of bedrooms that housed Miss Dennis and Rosemary when she was in residence. On this floor a studio had been built out on the west side, to get both view and light, and this added to the incongruous appearance of the house. On the floor above all the men slept, and here there were several vacant rooms. Freyne was supposed to sleep eighteen in comfort, though some of the cells had been converted into bathrooms, with the discovery of hygienic laws. The four of us—Bannister, Egerton, Dacre and I—had slept in adjoining rooms the previous night, the other side of the wing being closed, so that the step Miss Dennis had heard might have belonged to any of us, except for the lameness to which she testified. Above our rooms were the servants' quarters, in a long wing stretching out in an ungainly manner from the side of the house, like a clumsy chicken trying to extend her leg, and fearful of being nipped.

When the plan was complete Bradlaugh dismissed Miss Dennis and dealt with the rest of the party. They had nothing of any value to contribute. Rosemary remembered hearing Dacre go up to bed just before midnight with his dog; Bannister corroborated the story about comparing watches; otherwise he had nothing to say.

Bradlaugh had just finished that cross-examination when the lawyer arrived. I knew Mortimer fairly well; he was one of those fine-looking, aquiline men, well over sixty, with a foppish figure, very blue eyes and a pale skin. He was extraordinarily handsome, and exquisitely dressed: indeed, he was something of a dandy, with the blood of the Corinthians still warm in his veins. While he talked he played casually with a gold-rimmed glass on a wide ribbon of watered silk. He was shocked by the tragedy, but at first inclined to scoff at the notion of murder. As Bradlaugh finished his story, however, a sudden memory seemed to strike him, for he started, and then looked grave and troubled.

"Chandos made a new will quite recently," he said. "Up till then, there had been none since the early days of his marriage, when he left everything unconditionally to his wife and children. Last time I saw him—about six weeks ago—he told me he wanted to change it. Of course, he knew now there would be no children. That was a cruel blow to him. He was a very wealthy man, and his estate must be worth nearly a hundred thousand, even when the death duties have been paid. Originally this went to his wife, with certain restrictions about the children's share. Now she gets sixty thousand, on condition she does not remarry."

"Ah!" murmured Bradlaugh, "so he did mean what he said."

"There is nothing," Mortimer pointed out rather stiffly (for what is a detective to such a man, but a policeman in his Sunday clothes?) "to prevent Lady Chandos from marrying whom she chose."

"Except the loss of her inheritance, and that, in the particular instance foreseen by Sir Simon, is obstacle enough. Now for the rest of the will."

"It's perfectly straightforward. If Lady Chandos re-marries, Sir Simon's ward, Miss St Claire, comes into the bulk of the legacy, that is fifty thousand pounds. Lady Chandos retains the remaining ten, so that in any case she is provided for, regardless of her husband's means."

I broke in incredulously to ask how far he thought an income of five hundred pounds would go in paying Catherine's dress bills.

Mortimer, with a half-smile, murmured that so long as she remained unmarried she had three thousand a year, and that doubtless Chandos had argued that if she took a second husband he could make up the deficit. Then he went on, "In any case Miss St Claire gets ten thousand; Captain Dacre gets either ten thousand cash, or the cancellation of the debt on Dacre Court, if this has not been paid. Miss Dennis and Ravenswood get five thousand each; ten thousand goes to provide an Arts Scholarship, and the remainder, eight thousand odd, to various charitable institutions for children, and small legacies to servants."

He showed us the list of the children's homes that Chandos had selected; they were all hostels for the mentally defective, the blind, the crippled, and the incurables. To me, that last legacy was infinitely poignant, knowing how he himself had felt about children.

Bradlaugh, fortunately devoid of any sentimental impulses, asked unemotionally, "Do you know whether Sir Simon showed this to any one?"

"Presumably he would speak of it to his wife."

"But he never actually said so?"

"Not to me."

The detective turned in my direction. "And you?"

"He told me when I arrived that he wanted to discuss his will, but he didn't mention it last night. He thought the subject could keep."

"I wonder," Bradlaugh mused, "if Dacre could have had any inklings—through Lady Chandos, for example—and if that was what he meant when he said that Chandos' death might be advantageous to him. Otherwise the mortgage would pass with everything else to Lady Chandos. Or perhaps Miss Dennis has seen a draft, though she swears she hasn't."

"I know Miss St Claire knew nothing," Mortimer put in. "Chandos particularly told me that he didn't propose to saddle her even with so modest a fortune as this just yet. He said that if she married she should be free to choose some one who wouldn't want her for what she had." (Thus he had learned the bitter lesson of his own marriage. It was the only sign of cynicism I ever heard from him.)

"So I think you can count her out. As for the rest, I won't go surety. They may have been told, except, of course, Mr Ravenswood, who says he knew nothing."

"That complicates matters," Bradlaugh observed slowly. "There are so many people who might benefit from Sir Simon's death. His wife, from whom he was estranged, and who admittedly had her lover in the house; his ward, who is dependent on his generosity; his friend who was desperately in debt, and who was violently in love with Sir Simon's wife. . . ."

"The will doesn't help him," Mortimer cut in. "Directly Lady Chandos marries, she loses her income."

"It gives him Dacre Court, and from all accounts that meant a great deal to him. Then there is the secretary, who was in Sir Simon's confidence, knew about the morphia, and Sir Simon's early death."

"That should count her out," the lawyer suggested. "Knowing she had only a few months to wait. . . ."

But Bradlaugh said that that would provide an excellent basis for suicide, adding that there are some problems that will not wait even nine months.

CHAPTER 4 WHAT THE LIBRARY REVEALED

While Bradlaugh and his assistant, a tall sheep-faced man called Darbishire, carried out their investigation of the library, Mortimer and I sat in the hall, smoking innumerable cigarettes, and discussing this and that, but avoiding all talk of the murder. For Mortimer was a man of law, and he knew better than to set his cards on the table before the man who might, for aught he knew, be concerned with the crime.

Frobisher had telephoned that he would be along shortly; every one else was out of sight. Presently Mortimer fell silent and I also found myself with nothing to say. So we sat and listened to the mysterious sounds made by Bradlaugh and his aide-de-camp in the library. I didn't know by this time what I expected; the atmosphere tingled with possibilities, all unpleasant. But I scarcely think I should have been surprised to have discovered Bradlaugh's hand on my shoulder and Darbishire waiting with the handcuffs. Most of all was I reminded of a night I had once spent (for a dare-devil wager) in a well-known haunted house, and had remembered when the shadows grew thickest and I was most aware of my loneliness, except for "The Presences" of whom I had been warned, that peculiarly horrible story by W.F. Harvey called *The Beast with Five Fingers*. Every time the wind blew a branch against the pane I knew it was that monstrosity trying to get in.

Bradlaugh, of course, carried on without any of these half-human fears. He and Darbishire were like a pair of bloodhounds I had once seen on the track of an escaped convict—not in this country. Down on their knees on the library floor they examined every inch of the valuable Persian carpet, both with the naked eye and with magnifying glasses, as though the deep surface could retain footprints. Apparently their tirelessness was rewarded, for at last the door opened and the detective came over to me, with something small and dark in his hand.

"Have you ever seen this before?" he asked, showing it me.

I knew it at once. It was a small green seal, and I had last seen it at dinner the previous night on Dacre's watch-chain.

"Captain Dacre's watch-chain?" the man repeated. "What time was this? In the afternoon? Or later?"

I acknowledged reluctantly that I had not arrived until teatime, and had not noticed the seal until after the women had left us with the wine.

"After dinner, according to your evidence and that of other witnesses, all the men went upstairs together. Sir Simon was in your sight from that moment until you left him in the library at twelve-thirty?"

"He was in the room, of course. I can't swear that I kept my eyes on him all the evening."

"But you *can* swear that—between, say, eight-forty-five and twelve-thirty—the times when dinner was ended and you left Sir Simon for the night, he and Captain Dacre could not have been alone together *in that room*?"

"I can swear that."

"Then, clearly, Captain Dacre must have been here later."

But that was not my affair, and fortunately Frobisher arrived just then, and Bradlaugh turned towards him, explaining his theory.

"Injected?" growled the doctor. (He hadn't been able to save the small boy, who had died under the operation.) "Maybe. But you have to remember that he'd very likely taken a grain on his own account, and I've known cases where a grain was fatal."

"But not in the time," Bradlaugh urged. "It takes much longer for the symptoms to manifest themselves and for death to set in if it's taken in tabloid form. Besides, there are the missing tablets. According to Mr Ravenswood's evidence, there is much more than an additional half-grain missing."

Frobisher scowled again, and went upstairs. He told me later that he had never taken on a job he liked less. For he had liked Chandos very well. Bradlaugh went back to the library and began to examine the contents of the waste-paper basket. He took out the crumpled sheets we had seen that morning, smoothed them and began to read them carefully. There was, of course, a strong similarity between them. They were all addressed to Catherine. Presently he became quite still, like a dog pointing, and said in a puzzled voice, "There is something very strange here. These sheets were obviously thrown away as the writer found them inadequate: that is, they were creased and tossed into the basket in the heat of the moment. Yet not one of them is smudged, though they have never been blotted. The colour of the dry ink proves that. But what man carefully arranges spoiled sheets round him till they are dry and then destroys them?"

He picked up a pen that lay in the inkstand, dipped it in the pot, and scribbled half a dozen words at the foot of one of the sheets. These he blotted; the result was ink of a very pale colour, whereas the ink on the crumpled sheets was almost black. Then he took another sheet and wrote the same words again; these he allowed to dry. They dried a bright, hard blue.

"So that none of these sheets were written with this ink," said Bradlaugh. "Now for his fountain pen." But the question of that was easily settled; all of us could swear that the pen between Chandos' fingers had been the one that now lay in the ink-stand, a long, wine-coloured wooden holder, fitted with a relief nib. His pen was in his pocket, and this also had a relief nib. Bradlaugh tested it on a note-pad lying on the table. It wrote a clear blue-black when unblotted, and a rather lighter shade, that was quite dissimilar to the other blotted ink, when he put the blotting-paper on it.

"That seems to prove that these sheets weren't written in

this room at all," the detective said. "They were written with a different kind of ink, they were carefully allowed to dry, so as to save all tell-tale marks on blotting-paper, then they were creased and brought downstairs to lie here as evidence of suicide. Let's look at the paper."

He held it up to the light. The paper used had a smooth cream-laid surface; a pad of similar sheets was found in his drawer.

"It will be interesting to learn whether every room in the house is similarly provided," Bradlaugh murmured, laying it down. "Now we'll see what the blotting-paper has to tell us."

There was a pad of pink blotting-paper on the table, bound into a book of green leather, with the dead man's initials "S.C." stamped in gold. Bradlaugh began to examine it, sheet by sheet, with a precision that might have seemed painful to an amateur. Every scrap of writing that these betrayed was held over a mirror and carefully transcribed. Suddenly he stopped and taking up a pencil began to write down words and letters with dots between them, the whole occupying several lines of handwriting. Thereafter he re-wrote the message, filling in the gaps with the missing letters; and indeed, this was not difficult since so much was so clear. The complete fragment read like this:
—

". . . sorry you will not fall in with my plans. As you must realise, the position is a most unpleasant one for me, and unless you are prepared to agree with my suggestion I may find it necessary to take advantage of the mortgage I hold on Dacre Court. I feel sure, however, that you will not force my hand in this manner, and will make your apologies to my wife for your sudden change of plan."

Bradlaugh read that aloud, smiling grimly the while. "A new motive," he murmured, "and a side-light on Sir Simon's attitude. Interesting! This was written on the 20th. It is now the 22nd, so that Captain Dacre must have received it either late on the evening of Monday or, more likely, first thing Tuesday morning.

Not much notice, is it? And now, I think, we might with advantage interview Miss Dennis again."

He rang the bell, and a minute or two later Miss Dennis came down. Her eyes, crafty and suspicious, turned from one to other of her audience; her mouth closed like a trap. Behind those narrowed eyes was a mind that (like the mind of Mr Aden's hero) was like Clapham Junction that went all ways at once.

"There are one or two things, Miss Dennis, in which we think you can help us," Bradlaugh began suavely. "First, this paper." He held up a sheet. "Is it peculiarly Sir Simon's own, or is it distributed among his guests also?"

"Every room has paper and envelopes like that. I put them there myself."

"Then that won't help us. What about the ink? Is the ink in this well the same as that used by the guests?"

"I opened a new bottle yesterday, and filled all the ink-pots but this one, which wasn't half-empty. Sir Simon always uses a fountain-pen."

"And do all the guests who use the pens put out for them have the same sort of nib?"

Miss Dennis said they did: Chandos bought nibs in boxes of a gross.

"Then that won't help us either. One last point. Can you tell me Captain Dacre's precise movements yesterday from the time of his arrival?"

"Captain Dacre came down to lunch," she began, still speaking cautiously in case this was part of a campaign to make her commit herself irrevocably, though to what none of us knew then. "Immediately afterwards Sir Simon excused himself on the ground that he had a paper to write on the pre-Raphaelite school for the *Quarterly Art Review*. He had been collecting the material for some time, and he dictated the draft to me yesterday afternoon. Captain Dacre and Lady Chandos went out. We saw them pass the library window."

"You will swear on oath that Captain Dacre and Sir Simon did not have any opportunity for a few moments' conversation in here before the former went out?"

"Impossible. Sir Simon and I went straight from the lunch-table to the library, and he dictated for about two hours; then Mr Ravenswood came down and Sir Simon went upstairs for tea. Directly he left the drawing-room he called to me, and asked me to read over what he had dictated, and made a good many corrections. Then he asked me to get on with the work first thing in the morning. He didn't want me to do it last night, as he said I might prefer to be in the drawing-room. He didn't know how I hated that room, how it was tainted by Lady Chandos, till there didn't seem anything pure or lovely about it any more."

"And what time did he finish?"

"Just in time to dress. I saw him go upstairs, stooping rather because he had had a lot of pain in the afternoon; I stayed behind to clear up some of the books he had been using for reference. It doesn't take me long to dress; after all, no one was going to notice me." Outraged sex was rampant in her voice: but the man does not live who could have blamed Chandos for that.

Bradlaugh went on with a patience I was forced to admire. Neither her violent outbreaks nor the red herrings she drew across his path deterred him. That was the sort of man he was.

"And you left the library empty?"

"Yes, about twenty minutes before dinner; and I was down a quarter of an hour later making sure that everything was perfect in the dining-room."

"And Sir Simon?"

"He was down before any one else except Mr Egerton. They came down together, and they talked in the hall till Miss St Claire joined them. Then the others came down, and we had dinner. After dinner, as you have heard, Sir Simon went upstairs, and it was then . . ."

"Thank you, Miss Dennis, the rest of the story I know. Have you been with Sir Simon long?"

"Five years; ever since he bought this house."

"Ah! Beautiful old place. Elizabethan, isn't it?"

"Earlier than that," she said scornfully.

"Not this room, I think."

"Perhaps not this room," she conceded ungraciously, "but some of the original masonry, which you can see from the grounds—part of the small drawing-room, for instance—goes back to the twelfth century."

"An excellent refuge for runaways," Bradlaugh suggested. "Is there, by any chance, a secret passage leading out of this room?"

"I never heard of one. Oh, you're thinking of the key. But the windows...."

"Ah yes," he agreed gravely. "There are always the windows. Unfortunately, they are heavily shuttered, and the shutters fasten on this side. Every witness, including yourself, has said that those shutters were locked when the door was forced. It would be impossible to lock them from outside, and if there had been any attempt to tamper with them since the discovery of the body it would be bound to be noticed. The entire household cannot be concerned in the crime."

Miss Dennis, scarlet with embarrassment, blundered out of the room, and the bloodhounds got to work again. They examined the walls, testing every inch of the panelling, and every shelf of the bookcase, for signs of a secret way; they lifted down the big oil-paintings Chandos had hung over writing-desk and fireplace; they removed the tapestry that covered one side of the room; but they found nothing.

"The floor," said Bradlaugh curtly. They were still on their knees when I heard a door upstairs open, but as Frobisher reached the library Bradlaugh came to meet him, a curious light, denoting (with him) excitement in his eyes, and a square white envelope in his hand.

"You were right," said Frobisher in a sick sort of voice. "Injection. I've found the marks. The question of the exact quantity will have to wait till the autopsy. (In point of fact, the examination revealed about four grains of morphia in the body.) But I think you may take it it's murder all right. You have to remember he had already taken some of the stuff to deaden the pain before any low-down skunk came on the scene. So the odds are he was drowsy and only half-aware of what was happening. The murderer probably took advantage of that, and gave him no chance of realising the position. You noticed that when Chandos left the drawing-room he discarded his evening-jacket and got into a loose black velvet one, whose sleeve wasn't tight-fitting as regulation sleeves are. It would be the work of an instant to inject the stuff a little above the wrist, but not so high as is customary, then wait the short time before complete unconsciousness supervened, and afterwards prepare the stage. Now the question remains, what happened to the missing tablets?"

For answer Bradlaugh undramatically opened the envelope he carried, shaking it gently, so that its contents came up to the mouth.

"You recognise that?" he suggested.

Frobisher bent his leonine head. "Powdered morphine," he muttered. "Of course. The tablets crushed. Probably underfoot."

"How much is there there?"

Frobisher analysed it, and said presently, "About four grains. Roughly, that is. No doubt a little would be lost both in the pounding and the reassembling. Where did you come upon it?"

"Scattered haphazard on the bars of the fireplace and in the grate beneath. Of course the murderer never expected that the crime would be discovered, and even if it were he didn't think any one would take much notice of a fragment of white dust behind the brass tray in the fireplace. He wouldn't dare take the tablets with him in case he were seen on the stairs, and the alarm given; and if he ground it to powder and carried it off with him to dispose of later, he was laying himself open to the same risk, as some of it might easily adhere to his clothes. The needle must have been extraordinarily heavily charged."

Frobisher nodded. "Must have been. Then, having set the stage, you think he chose his moment and escaped upstairs?"

"Through a locked door?"

The doctor started. "So you haven't solved that mystery yet. Sure there's no other way out? What about the window?"

Bradlaugh patiently explained the difficulties presented by the window.

"Then it must be a secret passage."

"Ever heard of one?"

"Never. But, dammit, man, you can't expect a jury to believe that the fellow passed through a locked door."

"Quite. Personally, I share your sentiments. But both Lady Chandos and Miss Dennis assure me that they know nothing of any such thing. It would be very useful to know, beyond doubt, how many of the guests were aware that Sir Simon had morphia."

"I'm inclined to think the murderer didn't. He planned his dastardly plot, then discovered the tablets, saw the brilliant opening for suicide that it offered him. . . . Well?"

"Exactly. Next thing to learn is whether anybody in this house took morphia himself (or herself), or had access to it."

"I can tell you that," Frobisher returned instantly. "I can see soon enough whether you've a morpho-maniac on the premises."

He came to the door and opened it, and as he did so a man passed the door leading to the garden. Seeing us there, he hesitated a moment as if he would speak to us, then, changing his mind, began to move on. Frobisher, striding into the hall, hailed him in a voice that went pealing through that desolate house.

"Hallo, Dacre. I heard you were here. . . ."

"I don't doubt it," Dacre agreed with heavy sarcasm.

Frobisher held out his hand, and the other took it rather reluctantly. For about two minutes the doctor held his gaze. Then he spoke, and his voice was amazingly gentle—kind:—

"This is bad, Dacre," he said. "Since when have you taken to drugs?"

There was something very compelling about the tone and bearing. Dacre was already unnerved. Moreover, drugs eventually sap a man's will-power and moral sense, so that he was wax in Frobisher's hands. He yielded almost at once to the man's hypnotic influence, and answered his questions simply and without hesitation. His eyes had the appearance of a sleepwalker, glassy and vacant. He did not seem to realise that there was any one else there; perhaps we were out of his range of vision. But, be that as it may, he spoke as though he and the doctor were alone.

"This bloody war," he began in an odd, high voice, and then Frobisher set one hand on his shoulder.

"I know," he murmured soothingly. "I know. What was it? Nightmares? Terrors?"

Dacre, in the same sing-song voice, answered, "They never left me alone, waited until it was dark, and came back to me; you don't know. . . . Men mutilated, without heads, without hands, torn and raving, and starved, men who'd been dead for years, some of them. And they wouldn't let me sleep. When I tried they'd gather round the bed, and put foul fears into my mind. Then I dared not sleep. You remember the chap in Kipling's story who put a spur in his bed so that he shouldn't fall back and doze through sheer exhaustion, because of the horrors sleep brought? I've even done that. Till some one gave me morphia, and I slept, and they hadn't any power over me. Night after night—clean sleep."

"But not for long?"

Dacre's face changed. "No," he answered, and just as the man was a shadow of the devil-may-care healthy animal I'd known in France, so his voice wavered and grew shrill and thin. "Sometimes I couldn't get any peace no matter how greedily I took it to drive them away."

"Did you ever try anything else?"

"Anything that seemed to promise ease. There were so many things I wanted and couldn't have. I thought I was entitled to what I could take. But there are things one can't have—not if one starves. . . ." His voice trailed into silence.

I felt more sick then than I had done on that night in the haunted house; for Dacre had once been my friend. Frobisher put out one hand and caught the other man's left sleeve, pulling it up till I could see, for an instant, a terrible sight, an arm emaciated by privation and nervous strain, covered with needle-pricks. In certain spots these had become actual sores. It was clear that he had not been satisfied with half-measures. Then the doctor dropped the wrist he held, said, "Just a minute, my friend. I want to talk to you," and went back to Bradlaugh.

"If they bring a case against him," he said slowly, "I can testify that he's abnormal. I should hesitate to say absolutely insane, and I suppose nothing short of that would save him. But his isn't at the present time the intelligence of the average man. That amazing cunning, for instance, that is so richly evidenced in the setting of the crime; that quick yielding to hypnotic powers; the uncontrolled passions—he's literally incapable of holding himself in like an ordinary, decent man. . . . He gives himself away at every turn. It's the war, you know. I sometimes think the luckiest fellows are those who didn't come back. That chap cares for two things—Dacre Court, and Lady Chandos. She was out of his reach; Dacre Court was heavily mortgaged. Presumably he saw a chance of winning both by a certain bold stroke. That is the only defence to be urged for him, if the case against him is successful."

"If he's convicted nothing on this earth will save him from the gallows, unless he's detained at His Majesty's pleasure," Bradlaugh said grimly. "It's too infernally cold-blooded."

Frobisher nodded discontentedly, and went away. We could see him walking up and down with Dacre, talking in low tones. (He told me later that he was always more interested in the living than the dead, and Dacre at the moment offered a very fruitful field for speculation and research.) Bradlaugh continued his investigations, but though he still found no trace of the secret way, he did find something else that brought a new factor into the mystery. That was Chandos' cheque-book, and a counterfoil, dated 6th July, for a bearer cheque for six hundred pounds.

"That was while he was in town," Bradlaugh observed, and immediately I remembered Philpotts' story of the Woman in

Black.

CHAPTER 5 THE SPINNING OF THE NET

I

After the discovery of the cheque-book Bradlaugh locked the library and went upstairs to search the rest of the house. But on the first floor he seemed to meet with a check, for I heard him say in a cold voice, "Is there anything here that you are looking for, Mr Egerton?" All the doors having been sealed on the detective's arrival, there was no possibility of that young man going in or out of any of the rooms. But it would take more than a detective's hostility to move his habitual composure.

"Thank you. I have found it."

"And it was?"

"I wished to reassure myself that these boards were all polished."

Then he came casually downstairs and went in front of us into the garden. Dacre had disappeared and Frobisher came back and began to talk to Mortimer. After a moment I left the two together, and followed Egerton's example. The garden seemed deserted and chill, but Bannister, obviously ill-at-ease, was lingering alone by one of the flower-beds, examining a small purplish plant that grew in the borders. He straightened himself as I came up.

"Is it over yet?" I shook my head. "I believe these fellows regularly enjoy a man-hunt. Where are they now?"

I looked up; we were standing under the windows (two floors

above us) of the rooms we had occupied last night. Bannister's, Egerton's, mine and Dacre's—that was how they ran. I saw a shadow moving in the second room; then it disappeared as the detective crossed the floor and vanished from sight.

"Egerton's, isn't it?" I said a little doubtfully, for I had not troubled much about the location.

"Why should they start there?" Bannister asked suddenly. But I didn't know; for the police force is, by the grace of God, under the Crown, and services under the Crown are a law unto themselves.

Bannister hastened to change the subject. He felt his own position acutely. He found himself in a man's house—a man he had met for the first time two days earlier—amid a host of people who were all intimate; he was the sole outsider, and he felt shy of tacking himself on to any of the party. I was sorry for the man, and I encouraged his conversation on gardens to cover a mutual embarrassment.

"Lady Chandos has a very fine gardener," he observed. "I've seldom seen anything more magnificent than those apricot carnations. The Horticultural Society might be hard put to it to produce anything better. Does she exhibit, do you know?"

I said I believed not, and offered to show him the sunk garden Catherine had made. As we turned in that direction we caught sight of Rosemary and Egerton, and Bannister's manner changed suddenly.

"I wish you'd tell me," he said, colouring a little, "just how things stand. I feel like the Greedy Child on the wrong side of the sweet-shop window."

I said awkwardly, "As a matter of fact, I met Egerton for the first time yesterday...."

"I know about him," Bannister broke in. "He's Mountjoy's right hand, and he prophesies a brilliant future for him. He can afford to pitch away more brains than most of us possess and not miss the difference—much. His attitude in politics—and there are signs of his following in Mountjoy's footsteps and seceding to the Liberals—may carry considerable weight later. He's the type that's cut out for leadership."

"I didn't know we were entertaining angels unawares," I murmured, inexplicably disconcerted by the news. "Of course, I've heard his father's record."

"If you told young Egerton that he'd tell you that he agreed with H.G. Wells that one has to be a better man than one's father, or what's the good of successive generations? But—when I came down here—Miss St Claire was good enough to give me an invitation—I didn't, of course, realise quite how the thing stood. One's horribly afraid of—perhaps—saying the wrong thing, at such a time. Is there anything definite? I don't want to appear indiscreet or inquisitive.... Beastly word that."

"There's nothing definite," I said hesitantly, "but..."

"There soon will be—would be by now if it hadn't been for this appalling affair? I see. Oh well, it's just as I thought. They make a fine couple," but he sighed heavily as he said it.

I felt rather annoyed with Rosemary. She ought to have known better than to ask a man of his age and standing down to Freyne in order to hear her engagement announced to some other fellow. It wasn't like her, either. She was a fine sportsman, and she must have seen the chap was in love with her. But even girls like Rosemary don't understand how men feel about these things.

The more I thought about it the sorrier I was for him. He was pretty deeply in himself, and I couldn't help thinking what a brilliant match it would be for her. Bannister's name might not yet be numbered among the great of the earth, but it carried considerably more weight than Egerton's; as his wife Rosemary would have a goodly position, meet any number of people. Egerton's hopes for the future might be bright enough, but they all depended on Mountjoy, and there was a question whether he would be returned at the next Election. He was a Conservative, but he had leaned dangerously near the Liberal policy during the last Session, and there had been some awkward questions asked in his constituency. And though young Egerton was his right-hand man, he was only a cog in the older fellow's wheel, and when that wheel stopped spinning it seemed probable that Egerton would stop with it. Moreover, I couldn't make out that the fellow had any private means. His father had recklessly hurled away every penny that came to him, being cheated half the time, of course, but clinging to his last gasp to the fine ideal that it is better to be cheated by a thousand rascals than to distrust one honest man.

As I thus meditated we turned automatically in the direction of the sunken garden, Bannister following me; this garden is the pride of Catherine's heart, and is shut away from the rest of the grounds by a high hedge, cut into fantastic cherub-shapes.

We were lingering along by that hedge when we were startled by a voice—Dacre's voice.

"Catherine!" he cried, and I have never heard quite that timbre of agony in any man's tones before, "how could you throw yourself to the lions like that for me? Do you suppose I wouldn't a thousand times rather stand my trial for murder—even though Chandos was my friend—than hear what they'll say of you?"

"Ah, but *I* couldn't bear that," whispered Catherine.

"I'd have found some way out other than that," Dacre went on fiercely.

"What way?"

"I can't tell you now—I don't know."

"There was no other way. And Rupert . . ." here her voice fell low and caressing and fearless as Chandos would have staked all his fame to hear it, "as if I care! I would have told them what I did a million times rather than one hair of your dear head should be hurt."

Dacre said in a choked voice, "I care."

"For yourself? Or for me? Am I less to you because of what people know of us, think of us?"

"As if I could do other than worship you for what you have done for me today," he cried bitterly.

He was a man on the rack, and Bannister and I instinctively avoided one another's eyes. We were in the curve of the V-shaped hedge, and a movement in either direction meant revealing ourselves. "You've tossed away your reputation, cut yourself adrift from your world. . . . I didn't know you cared like that. Do you suppose you'll find it worth while at the end?"

"I have no world but you," said Catherine simply. Bannister gave a convulsive start, as who should protest against the violent indecency of our presence there, and in so doing dislodged a pebble that struck me sharply on the ankle. Taken unawares I muttered something, and immediately there was a sharp movement on the other side of the hedge, and Catherine and Dacre came into view.

It was an embarrassing moment. But Catherine recovered herself first, and said in tones of forced gaiety, "Have you brought Mr Bannister to see the sunk garden?"

I said wretchedly, avoiding her eyes, that I had, and she, making casual conversation, led us towards the place, with its irregular beds and lily-pond and its inevitable sundial.

Bannister made adequate comments. I slipped round to Dacre's left, and tried to minimise the horrible awkwardness that lay upon us all. In that moment I admired Catherine so much that I even forgot her cruel disloyalty to Chandos.

"I must show you my frogs," I heard her say to Bannister, who masked his discomfort better than either of us. She stooped and put her hand in the pool, bringing it out an instant later with a smart young frog in green and yellow, who, quite untroubled, sat placidly on her hand, his yellow waistcoat panting contentedly.

Something in Dacre seemed to snap. "How can you let that cold-blooded monstrosity touch you?" he cried. Both Catherine and Bannister were taken aback. The frog leaped into the pool again with a splash.

"He's a darling," she said, covering up her surprise, "I only wish I could show you the father of all the frogs. He's enormous and very dignified, but he will sit on the very bottom of the pool, where it's much too deep for me to get him."

Bannister said something else, and we waited a moment, all of us thoroughly aware of the impossible situation. Catherine must have known that we had overheard part at least of her conversation with Dacre. He himself was anxious to break up the group, but words never came gracefully to his lips. It was Bannister, that polished man of the world, who eventually found the right thing to say, and we sheered off, feeling uncommonly blackguardly. I said nothing. Dacre's eyes haunted me.

As we came into the house Bradlaugh met us with a question on his lips.

"Have you seen Lady Chandos anywhere?"

"I believe," said Bannister, "that she is down by the sunken garden." Neither of us offered to find her, but just as the silence became oppressive, and both of us feared that Bradlaugh would himself go in search, and in his turn, overhear her crazy indiscretions, she came into sight, Dacre still at her side. Rosemary and Egerton followed at some distance, deep in conversation. They seemed to have put the immediate tragedy behind them, as befitted their years. But when I saw the look that flashed into Bannister's face I felt horribly sorry for him.

Then my thoughts were dragged back rudely to Chandos' affairs. The detective was questioning Catherine again.

"You told me this morning, Lady Chandos, that Captain Dacre was with you between the hours of twelve-forty-five and five o'clock?"

"A little later than five."

"And you were sure of that because you kept an eye on the clock beside your bed?"

"Yes."

"I have examined your room with the rest, and naturally I observed the clock. This is it?" He drew out of his pocket a pale blue folding travelling clock, with luminous hands and dial.

Catherine seemed puzzled and apprehensive. "Yes."

There was neither triumph nor accusation in the detective's voice as he replied, "You will note that it stopped at 12.25 a.m. It is now 12.15. Obviously it was not wound last night."

Catherine was too much taken aback to invent any lie that would hold water; I doubt, even if she had been warned, if she could have brazened it out. It was simple to read Bradlaugh's suspicions. Possibly Dacre had been to her room, but there was nothing to show that it had been before the hour that Chandos was murdered. Catherine had chosen the earliest and latest possible times for his coming and going, in order to clear him finally from suspicion. Her voice, however, at that stage, betrayed less fear than anger. She was scornful of her carelessness in not having made certain that her case was perfect, but she was not afraid of Bradlaugh because he had made the discovery.

"I can only repeat what I have already said," she told him. "It is unfortunate that the clock should not support me, but the fact remains in spite of it."

All through the detective's cross-examination, all through the interminable business of the inquest next day, she clung to her story. But Bradlaugh's discovery had raised a new doubt in our minds. Dacre might have gone to her room, but in any case Catherine was desperately afraid he was guilty of murder. She would willingly commit perjury to save him. She had forgotten Chandos; she could do nothing to help him now, and it seemed obvious to me that all her energies were turned on saving her lover.

But Bradlaugh was building up a wall of evidence round the fellow, brick by brick, steadily, unerringly. The search of the house gave him a fistful of evidence, that began with the ominous presence of the seal in the library.

"I noticed nothing last night," Dacre said sullenly, "but then I had no reason to look for it."

"And this morning?"

"The house was already dark with rumours. I dressed hastily; possibly I should have discovered it during the day."

"It was seen on your watch-chain at dinner-time; according to your own evidence you did not see Sir Simon again before his death, neither did you enter the library."

"It may easily have slipped its moorings during the *tamasha* of this morning."

"I understand from witnesses that at no time during the morning did you come sufficiently far into the room to have dropped the seal on the farther side of the fireplace, where it was found."

A new, ugly look came into Dacre's eyes. "And who has been good enough to say so?"

But Bradlaugh was no more intimidated by his anger than he had been by Catherine's scorn. "I have the evidence of more than one witness; in cases like these the smallest detail is of importance."

"No doubt," he sneered. He was trying to discover the end of the perilous road he was travelling; so far as he and the rest of us could guess it ended with a gibbet. Then he grew livid and his voice broke out, horrible and violent. "It's a plot, a damned plot to get rid of me. I never went near his room in the night, never laid a finger on him. Why should I? What did I gain from his death?"

"Dacre Court," said Bradlaugh slowly.

Dacre started. "What do you mean?"

"You may not know, perhaps, that under Sir Simon's will you receive the cancelled mortgage on your property."

Dacre's face whitened. "He did that?"

"Yes."

The other man seemed to be trying to find his feet. "But even so," he burst out, "what did it profit me? He wasn't going to take up the mortgage if he lived."

"You're sure?"

"Of course. He didn't need the money."

"He had suggested, hadn't he, that you should go abroad, and not come down here again?"

"What the devil's that to do with the case?" Dacre flamed.

"The jury may think it very important. I take it that it is true?"

"I had to see him on business affairs. I wrote to tell him so."

"And he answered?"

"He didn't answer. I swear he didn't." But his eyes were all the time searching the detective's face.

"And if we can produce a facsimile of the letter he sent you saying that unless you agreed to his suggestion he would take steps to realise his mortgage on Dacre Court—what then?"

Dacre surprised us all by a wild shout of laughter. "He wouldn't do such a thing. You may not have known him, but I did, and I can assure you he wasn't a blackmailer."

"And if, as I say, we can prove he did write such a letter?"

Dacre's laughter died, his face changed, grew gray, ashen with fear. He was seeing himself as a man furiously beset on all sides, with no one to give him a hand through the thicket.

He uttered a bitter oath. "It's what I told you—it's a plot, an infernal plot...."

It was the effect of drugs, no doubt, reacting on the fellow's shattered nerves, but it was a sight from which we all recoiled. It is not nice to see a man go to pieces, all his morale crumbling. Dacre was shaking with terror. I was only thankful that Catherine was not there.

II

Bradlaugh was quite unmoved. Without further noticing Dacre's state of mind he produced two letters, the first from Chandos, clearly the letter of which Miss Dennis had spoken, and the second from Catherine, of whose existence none of us had hitherto guessed.

Chandos' was typical of the generosity and sympathy of the man.

"MY DEAR DACRE,—I gather from Catherine that she is including you in her invitations for the 21st. You will, I am sure, not misunderstand me, when I say I am certain you would be wise to refuse. We are all aware of the unfortunate position in which we find ourselves, and in these circumstances it would, surely, be nothing less than madness to come down here again and needlessly torture yourself.

"If I may be so far presumptuous, I would suggest that you leave England for a time, until the tension has somewhat

relaxed. If finance presents difficulties I shall be glad to lend a hand. Should you agree to this, I will undertake to see that Dacre Court comes to no harm in your absence. I know you will feel very strongly about letting it to strangers."
"Sincerely yours,
"SIMON CHANDOS."

After that it seemed incredible that any man could be so far lost to good taste as to disregard such an appeal. Chandos must have put his own pride very far out of sight before he could bring himself to write it. But before any of us could speak, Bradlaugh brought out the second letter.

"Rupert, my dear, I believe Simon is writing to ask you not to come here. He knows our secret, and of course it has hurt him. But haven't we been hurt too? Rupert, if ever you loved me, come down now. Things are intolerable, and I can't bear it much longer. Five years, almost six.... My life is so short, just the hours I am with you. I've fought against admitting that ever since that day, two years ago—you remember? But I can't help it now. I've had to live on a memory of you for five months. Let me have another day or two of you in the flesh...."

I think our feeling was unanimous that, if the situation was so abhorrent to her, Catherine should have done the honourable thing and asked Chandos for a divorce. But when she was confronted with that question she lifted her colourless, stricken face and said, "He wouldn't give it me. I begged him—once. I couldn't endure that again. Rupert and I would have told him..."

"This morning?"
"Yes—unless..."
"Unless what?"
"We had decided to take our own future into our hands before he could separate us. We knew we should never belong, if he could prevent us."

Dacre, faced with the letters, did not attempt to deny the

source of either. He had received Chandos' first, but before he could answer it Catherine's had reached him, and he had flung discretion and honour and loyalty to the winds, and come down to Freyne.

"But he says nothing of Dacre Court," he pointed out excitedly.

"That was the third letter," Bradlaugh answered, and none of Dacre's vehement denials moved him.

But even without that letter the case against the man warranted his arrest. For in his room was found the hypodermic syringe he habitually used, together with a larger supply of morphia, according to Frobisher, than any man, bar a doctor, has a right to possess.

"It shouldn't be possible for him to lay hands on it," he confided to me. "No doctor gives a prescription for that amount, or a quarter of it. Besides, we're so careful now. I've known a chemist refuse to make up a doctor's order unless he added a note that it was to be made up once only."

"Then how does he get it?"

"There are half a hundred illegal ways. A woman came to see me the other day. Said she had met me at Chelmsford, at the house of a Professor Darby. It's true Darby is an old college friend of mine, but I didn't recall her. But then one meets so many people.... So I said vaguely that I was glad to meet her, and waited to know what I could do. She chatted for a bit, then said she was staying in the place for a few weeks, and asked me if I remembered the prescription I gave her at Chelmsford. I said I was afraid not, and she laughed and went on, 'Oh, but you must, doctor, The one with morphia in it.' I rang the bell and had her shown out. I heard afterwards she'd carried a similar story to every doctor within a radius of five miles. They're as hard pushed for it as that. However, I don't say Dacre got his that way. Probably he knows some secret trafficker. Must, I should say, judging from the quantity. The latest way is to send cocaine packed between the boards of playing-cards. There's a bridge club in London that exists for no other reason than to sell packs to its members. Fifty-three cards yield quite a nice little amount.

Dacre's probably in a similar net. I don't like the look of the man. I should like to certify him insane, but I daren't quite do it. He's suffering from repression of some sort, and it's reacting on his nerves and his brain. His own story that he's been hopelessly in love with Lady Chandos for fifteen years is quite enough to account for that."

I glanced round furtively. There was no one to be seen. Then I asked, "If it isn't unfair to you, doctor, do you think there's a chance he did do it? We shan't hurt him by discussing it for an instant here, particularly in view of his physical condition."

"I should say it's quite possible," said Frobisher without hesitation. "But if he did, and the case is brought against him, he'll swing for it, as sure as Fate. And yet it'll be damned unfair. In his right mind he'd be incapable of such a thing. That's why I'm heart and soul against the death penalty. It hangs men who are technically guilty and morally innocent. Dacre at the moment is in the grip of mania; but free him from his complex where Lady Chandos is concerned, give him the chance of a normal life, and he'd be a different man and probably an excellent citizen. I suppose that wound in the forehead troubles him sometimes, particularly in scorching weather like this. This steamy rain is worse than all the sun."

For the moment we left it like that. I went back to the library, and found Bradlaugh still looking at the cheque-book.

"I'm going up to town this afternoon," he said, "I'll try to get the evening train back. I want to see the manager of Sir Simon's bank. I'm going to 'phone him now to wait for me in case I get hung up. I don't like the look of that cheque."

I felt that, in so much darkness, any man who had a match ought to strike it and shed what illumination he could. So I said reluctantly (for I didn't want Chandos' name dragged through the mud on his own account as well as Catherine's). "There's just one thing you should know that conceivably has something to do with that cheque," and then I told him Philpotts' story.

"When was this?"

"When he was up in town seeing the specialist, presumably."

"In these cases we don't presume. We confirm," snapped Bradlaugh.

"I might get him on the telephone," I suggested. "Though it's doubtful if he'll remember the actual day."

"Would he recognise the woman again?"

"I'll ask him."

Bradlaugh got through to the manager shortly afterwards, and while we waited for my call the detective said, "Have you any reason to suspect that there was some secret in Sir Simon's life? Anything that would account for this woman?"

"Emphatically—never."

By excellent good fortune I got Philpotts at his club. His voice, even over the wires, was agitated and shocked.

"I say, old man, what's all this yarn about Chandos being poisoned? Shouldn't have thought he was that sort of bird at all. One thing, I'll bet that damned woman's at the bottom of it."

"That's what I've rung you up about. Can you remember exactly when you saw them together?"

"'Bout three weeks ago, I should say."

"I mean, the actual date? It would help us a good deal if you could verify it."

Philpotts thought. "It was the day I went up to see my lawyer-feller," he said at last. "Might have a note in my diary." He set down the receiver and began to search for it. Over the wire I could hear sundry grunts and curses; then a silence so long that I thought he had disappeared. After that Exchange tried to cut us off, and I had just succeeded in pacifying them when Philpotts came through again.

"Had the deuce of a job finding it. Yes—July 6th—a Monday."

"Thanks, old man. What time of day?"

"Oh—about half-past eleven—twelve—sometime before lunch."

"I see. And do you think you'd know her again?"

"Oh well—pretty tall order, old son. But yes. I might. She leaned forward in the cab and I got a good squint at her. Didn't want to look twice. Most malevolent woman I ever saw, and that's saying a lot. Still, I'd be glad to help get her put where she can't break up another fellow's life."

"Do you mean to tell me she and Chandos were casually driving through London? He isn't altogether unknown, you know, and no one could possibly have mistaken her for his wife."

"Casual? There wasn't anything casual about Chandos, believe me. The poor devil sounded about broken up. Why, no man in his senses would want to be found with a woman like that unless he were anxious to see the inside of a gaol. I reckon Chandos was up against it good and hard before he shared a taxi with her."

"Where did you see them?"

"By Charing Cross. The road was up as usual, and my taxi got jammed cheek by jowl with theirs."

"Did you hear anything?" I asked, suddenly inspired.

"I heard this. Chandos said, 'You'll swear this is the only one you had?' and she answered that if she'd had more she'd have put 'em up for sale. And then my taxi jolted me off down Northumberland Avenue. Rum thing how often you're mewed up in a damn' dull conversation for hours, and can't get away, and then, other times you're dragged off by the ear the second it gets interesting."

"Tell your friend," Bradlaugh cut in, "that I'll be coming to see him when I'm through with the Bank." So I gave him the message and hung up the receiver.

"The only one?" I repeated. "Only what?"

"Letter, I should imagine," the detective answered dryly. "It would help a good deal if we had some idea of the subject-matter. I doubt if Lady Chandos would know, and I'm not anxious to confront her with possible unfortunate episodes in her late husband's career unless and until it's absolutely necessary. I'm off now; my train goes in twelve minutes."

He came back late that night without having learned very much more. The manager remembered Chandos' visit perfectly; he had seemed very much exhausted and a little unnerved. His manner was as courteous as always, but his hand had shaken a little as he counted the notes. They had been ten-pound notes.

"Less easy to trace," observed Bradlaugh caustically. He had called alone with the cheque on the morning of the 6th July, about eleven-fifteen.

The manager had seen him, and afterwards had watched him get into a taxi. There had been someone else in the taxi, he thought, a woman, but he did not observe her closely. He had taken it for granted that it was Lady Chandos, whom he had never seen. He did not obtain a clear view of her at all. She was dressed in black, he thought. In any case, he had had an appointment with a man who had asked the Bank to purchase for him a very large quantity of oil shares, and was going abroad the following day. There had been various matters to settle, a power of attorney to be granted, and so forth, and he had not had much time for idle conjectures concerning Simon Chandos. It was the first time he (Chandos) had ever drawn a bearer cheque for such an amount. The manager had himself been surprised, since the man's cheque must have been acceptable anywhere.

Bradlaugh managed to get the numbers of the notes and then went on to Philpotts' club. But E.P. couldn't help him much.

"Your friend's experience of women appears to have been very extensive," said the detective unsmilingly to me on his return, "including the blackmailing type. Still, it won't be easy to locate this woman. We know nothing of her, her name, her business, her possible relation to Sir Simon. However, for the moment we must mark time."

"She could hardly have been here last night," I suggested.

"There is such a thing as collusion," Bradlaugh reminded me sharply. "I don't doubt that if we had more information about her, we should be so much the nearer to our solution. It will be necessary, unless a proven case is brought against any one in this household, to follow up this blackmailing woman's tracks. The numbers of the notes may help us."

But all the same I could see that he regarded it as a forlorn hope.

CHAPTER 6 THE VERDICT

I

The inquest, held at Freyne Abbey the next morning, brought a new factor into the case. For the first time it was quite clearly suggested that the whole affair was a case of collusion between Catherine and Dacre. Althea Dennis set the ball rolling by mentioning, quite gratuitously, that at the time when Chandos was in London, learning the specialist's verdict, Catherine had been also away from Freyne, though not with her husband.

"Did she tell you why?"

"She said she was tired, and wanted a complete rest."

"A more complete rest than she could find in a quiet spot like Freyne Abbey?"

Miss Dennis' lips curled. "Presumably."

"She left an address, of course?"

"The Golden Swan Hotel, Daisycombe—not far from Dacre Court. But no doubt she could explain her motives better than I."

The jury pricked up their twenty-four ears. Something sensational was afoot; they waited with eagerness for Catherine's evidence. They were composed of five neighbouring landowners and farmers, and seven tradesmen, with some of whom Catherine habitually dealt. The Coroner was a wordy, solid man called Waltham, who made no secret of his views. The cross-examination to which he made Catherine submit was the depths of degradation. She had suffered enough, Heaven knew, under Bradlaugh's fusilade; but she had come out of that with her courage still held high. But under this man she flagged momentarily; her answers were so faint that more than once he forced her to repeat them. He seemed to think that, could he prove the liaison to be one of some duration, half his work was done.

"In your letter to Captain Dacre you refer to an episode of two years ago. What was that?"

There was some protest at the question, but he beat it down. "It's highly important," he fussed, "to show that there were good reasons for wishing the dead man out of the way. We are here to learn the truth, in any ways we can." And he asked the question again.

"When I admitted that—I cared for him." Her reply was so wan that even the jury murmured among themselves, passing the words from lip to lip.

"And how long has he been your lover?"

Catherine half-turned and shot an appealing glance at Dacre, who was sitting hunched in his chair; his face was pinched like the face of a dead man; the lips were livid; only his eyes seemed alive, smouldering fires in the waste lands of his face.

The coroner rapped out the query for the second time. "And how long..."

"Never—until that night," whispered the tortured woman inaudibly. Waltham pooh-poohed that, and proceeded with a brutality that verged on indecency.

"And yet, as soon as your husband leaves Freyne for London, you take the opportunity of going away also, unattended even by your maid?"

"I wanted a change of air, and it seemed a good time, when my presence at Freyne was not really needed."

"What made you select Devonshire?"

"I like the county. I have frequently stayed there before."

"At Daisycombe?"

"Not always at Daisycombe, but in the neighbourhood."

"Always within—say, ten miles of Daisycombe?"

Catherine looked puzzled and frightened. She suspected a trap, but could not place it. "Y-yes, I think so."

"I suggest to you, Lady Chandos, that you invariably chose that neighbourhood because it is comparatively close to Dacre Court."

She broke into shuddering denials. "No—no. In all the time I was there I only saw Captain Dacre once."

"And when was that?"

"Two years ago."

"The occasion referred to in the letter?"

"Yes."

"And yet—realising your danger—you deliberately chose to return again and again to the neighbourhood, even though you knew that Captain Dacre was in residence, and would possibly, even probably, know where you were staying?"

"I never told him," she whispered through bloodless lips.

The coroner was openly sceptical. "And the other occasions when you visited Devonshire? Was your husband always away?"

"Usually. Otherwise we went away together. It was only when he had to see about some picture being hung or something of that kind that I went away, too."

"And he knew of it?"

"Certainly."

"Knew that you had chosen a neighbourhood where the man whom you loved was living?"

All Catherine's self-possession seemed to have deserted her at last. She could find no adequate answers to his questions. Only at the end did she fire up a little, lifting her head. "Why should I want to kill my husband in order to marry the man I loved? On my re-marriage all my fortune goes to some one else." But even that didn't serve her, for the coroner countered, "But earlier in your evidence you swore that you had not seen the will, and knew nothing of its contents."

From what I could gather from the atmosphere of the Court he was winning all along the line. The prevailing impression seemed to be that Catherine had known of the earlier will, whereby she inherited all Chandos' possessions, and that she had murdered him to achieve a double purpose. Now she discovered to her dismay that both were out of her reach.

With the calling of Dacre the case steadily deteriorated. He also was asked the period during which he had been Catherine's lover. His immobility broke down suddenly, and an agonising new life came back to his numbed limbs.

"I have never been her lover," he cried wildly. "If it had not be for certain important matters I had to discuss with Sir Simon I should not have gone to Freyne at all."

"Why not?"

If the question was unexpected so was the answer. "Because he was my friend."

"And you deny absolutely . . ." the coroner scoffed.

Without warning Dacre's control broke. "Prove it," he shouted, "prove it to this or any other court that at the time when Lady Chandos was out of town she was with me. Prove it, I say. Then, but not till then, bring your charge against me. There's not a word of truth in the accusation."

"I believe it is a fact that at the time mentioned by Lady Chandos you were actually in residence at Dacre Court?"

"I don't keep a diary showing exactly where I spend each day."

"No doubt your servants could help us."

"No doubt they could," the hunted man sneered. "As a matter of fact, with the exception of certain weekends, very few and far between, I haven't been away from Dacre Court for more than two years."

"And the occasion to which Lady Chandos refers in her letter?"

"I was unaware that she was staying in the neighbourhood, till we chanced to meet in the countryside."

"And you made love to her?"

"I admit I lost my head. It was the unexpectedness of the meeting. It could never have happened in her husband's house."

Waltham smiled disagreeably. "And then?"

"We realised, of course, the impossibility of the position. I did not see her again till her return to town."

"And her second reference about seeing you five months ago?"

"That was when she and Sir Simon were spending a short time in London, and I had chanced to come up to see a man about some dogs I was breeding for him. I met Sir Simon in the street, and he asked me to come to dinner the same night. There were no other guests, and I was not alone with Lady Chandos at any time during the evening."

"Really! Now, to come to the next point. The morphia. Can you explain how you come to have such a large quantity?"

"Dr Frobisher will tell you that I use large quantities of morphia for my own needs."

"And you brought the syringe down with you?"

"Certainly. I can't sleep without it, and sometimes not even then."

They could get nothing out of him as to the source of the drug; but conversely, he could not explain the presence of the seal in Chandos' room. He denied once again that he had received the third letter containing the threat to Dacre Court, nor could Miss Dennis find any note of it in her posting-book. It transpired, however, that on the afternoon of the 20th she had been out for some hours, and it was probable that Chandos, anxious to catch the London post—and at Freyne collections are few and far between—went out himself and dropped it in the box.

The case against Dacre was black enough when he stood down, but my testimony unwittingly made it worse. For the coroner put the question that Bradlaugh had either overlooked or deliberately kept for a more fitting occasion.

"Mr Ravenswood, you were the last to admit to seeing the dead man during his lifetime. Did he say anything that made you believe he was aware of any intrigue between his wife and Captain Dacre?"

"Nothing." I could, at any rate, answer that honestly.

"He said nothing that pointed towards suspicions on his part against a third party in his domestic affairs?"

It is a thankless job to stone a drowning man, but I recalled with dismay Chandos' fierce accusations.

"He was, of course, aware of Captain Dacre's attachment to Lady Chandos."

"And he viewed it with complacence? Really, sir, you can hardly ask us to accept that."

"It caused him considerable anxiety," I retorted a shade acidly.

"Then he regarded it with marked disfavour? Knowing as he did how short a time he had to live did he say anything that might lead you to think that after his death he would approve, or even not actually disapprove, of a marriage between his wife and Captain Dacre?"

"He was whole-heartedly against it," I admitted.

"Did he tell you why?"

"It is known that Captain Dacre's health is very poor," I said feebly.

"So that his objections were based on purely physical grounds?"

"I don't think he cared much for the idea, apart from that."

"And his reasons?"

There was no help for it, and though I toned down Chandos' actual words, they were pretty damning. Dacre's face slowly lost its faint flicker of hope as I finished.

"And in your experience of him, was Sir Simon a man who made such charges lightly?"

"By no means."

"Have you ever known him prefer a charge against a man and not be justified by events?"

"Never, so far as my memory serves me."

Here a juryman, who inclined towards the theory of Dacre's innocence, asked sharply, "Isn't it strange that the man who said such harsh things of Captain Dacre should, on his own showing, have offered to help him a few days earlier?"

The coroner said tolerantly, "Most of us can be friendly when there's a chance of getting an undesirable neighbour out of the way. As long as he thought he might be successful he was prepared to help; but when it became clear that Captain Dacre defied his precautions, he turned ugly. And in any case, future events proved him justified once again."

There was a sharp intake of breath from the listeners. "He hasn't proved Rupert did it yet," Rosemary muttered to Egerton. I heard Egerton whisper back, "He's referring to Lady Chandos' evidence."

"And will they try and say that Catherine...?"

"Not they," Egerton scoffed. "No actual evidence of complicity. But they'll bring in against Dacre."

And they did.

The coroner rose and drew for us a picture of the deliberate crime. He showed us Dacre and Catherine spending the afternoon together, carefully preparing the scheme, testing it to make sure that it was water-tight; then the stage carefully set for the public insult offered to the husband; Dacre going off to bed early on a plea of a savage headache; Lady Chandos carefully listening at a half-closed door for the sound of steps, counting the ascent of her guests; a stealthy footstep about one o'clock when they might be expected to be asleep; the cautious creeping down the stairs, the tap on the library door, possibly a suggestion that the important matters referred to be discussed there and then, since Dacre would say that he did not care to remain long at Freyne; the vile advantage taken of an exhausted and suffering man; the carefully watched-for opportunity, the swift stab of the needle, the callous pause till unconsciousness supervened, the preparation of the crumpled sheets, the letter written and set in front of the dead man, the pen placed in the still warm hand—and the blunder irrevocably made. If the murderer had discovered his mistake the next morning when he entered the library, he must have hoped that the rest of the household would be equally oblivious to the grave evidence it bore against him. Possibly even, when the room was empty, he would have changed the position of the pen: it had been only Mr Egerton's sharp observation that had enabled them to discover the crime at all. Then, having locked the door and put the key in the dead man's pocket, he had left the room by a secret exit, and (probably) made his way up to his accomplice's room. That, however, was a matter for conjecture and did not materially affect the case.

The jury were greatly moved. They were absent a very short time. On their return they declared, "We find the deceased to have died of morphine poisoning, injected subcutaneously, and we bring in a verdict of wilful murder against Rupert Dacre."

They shot malevolent glances at Catherine, but she was too much aghast and defeated by the result of the inquest to care. For an instant I dreaded a scene; then Catherine, with the dignity she had shown during that first appalling morning at Freyne, rose and dropping her veil over her face left the impromptu court.

II

Later, Egerton suggested a foursome. "The fewer people here to madden Lady Chandos the better," he said. "We can do nothing except take ourselves decently out of the way. Tomorrow we shall be able to get back to town."

So Bannister and I played Rosemary and Egerton. I was out of practice, and I could not for an instant banish from my mind the tragic picture of Catherine learning what her motions of love and loathing had done to the two men who mattered the most in her life. Bannister was a crack player and Egerton even better.

Rosemary, like me, was off her game, but in the end she and Egerton won by a brilliant stroke of that young man's.

Bannister and I walked back slowly together, the others being some distance ahead.

"A wonderful putter, that lad," Bannister remarked thoughtfully. "I should say it's a habit with him."

"Putting?" I asked mechanically, my thoughts busy with the man who lay dead at Freyne, and the other who had been charged with his murder.

"No. Winning any game he sets his hand to." I pulled myself together sufficiently to realise that he was thinking of Rosemary and had no hope at all.

I lingered a minute or two in the hall after we got in, so that I didn't immediately follow the others upstairs. When I did ascend, the staircase was empty. As I passed the small drawing-room the door opened, and Catherine stood on the threshold. I stopped dead in sheer horror. Her eyes had a terrible glassy look, as if she had been drugged. She was wearing something colourless, but not more so than her face. She had hitherto resembled a fluttering candle wavering in the draught of a great fear; now she was the same candle extinguished, guttered, misshapen. Even her voice was ashy with misery.

"They've taken him, Alan," she whispered. "Taken him for what he never did."

I realised then how wise Egerton had been in his suggestion that as few of us as possible should be present at the humiliating and pitiable scene of Dacre's arrest.

CHAPTER 7 A NEW TRAIL

I

We stayed at Freyne till noon of the following day in order to attend Chandos' funeral. Catherine refused to go; in any case she would have been wiser to remain behind closed doors, but Dacre's removal had broken her up absolutely. I think, right up to the end of the inquest, she had believed some miracle would be performed and he would be saved. When he was actually charged with murder, horror and misery overwhelmed her. So I went as her representative, and Rosemary came with me, Rosemary, very pale and erect and tearless, though I knew how much she had loved the dead man. She wouldn't carry flowers or consent to take any on Catherine's behalf to be tossed into the grave and be crushed by clods.

"Why must you kill beauty because something else that was once beautiful has died?" she demanded. I think we were all moved by that word "beautiful" in connection with Chandos. It struck straight to Catherine's heart.

"What is it in me that makes me dead and blind where every one else is alive?" she whispered in anguished tones. "A child like Rosemary saw him as beautiful, while I . . ." She covered her face with her hands.

I couldn't point out to her that Rosemary hadn't been his wife, so I said nothing. Bannister and Egerton followed in another cab, presumably because Rosemary was there. I didn't think either of them could mourn Chandos sufficiently to go for any other reason. Behind them came the servants, except Peters, Lady Chandos' maid, who stayed behind to tend her mistress; while most of the village turned out for the occasion, standing a respectful distance from the grave.

As soon as the funeral was over we came up to town. Rosemary went to stay with a friend of hers in South Kensington; Catherine and Peters reopened the little flat in Mayfair that Chandos had kept going for his wife's convenience, Bannister went back to his rooms, I settled in my club; I didn't know where Egerton or Althea Dennis went.

I had promised Catherine to do what I could with regard to getting legal defence for Dacre when his trial came on. I knew Vincent Herringham, and I thought I might be able to get him to take up the case. There seemed no particular hurry. It would not be called before mid-September at the earliest, and it was hard to believe that, after Bradlaugh's tooth-combing process at Freyne, any fresh evidence was procurable. Too minute a search, I feared, might reveal the fact that Catherine and Dacre had been lovers intermittently during the past two years, and that would prejudice his case. On the other hand, I failed to see how he could prove the contrary. Anyway, it was of the utmost importance that he should have the best possible advice.

"He'll need it," said Egerton dryly, as we parted at Charing Cross.

I failed to get Herringham, and that depressed me a good deal. The opinion of such a man was valuable, and it made me doubt Dacre more than I had done hitherto when he said in his short decisive way, "Nothing doing, Ravenswood." A day or two later I got a card from him. "Try Wareing; forlorn hopes are his speciality. Tell him I sent you." That same afternoon I came by chance on Bannister in Pall Mall. We exchanged greetings and then he said a shade diffidently, "Has anything been done yet about Dacre? I mean—he'll defend the case, of course, that is, if he can stand the racket. Life seems pretty cheap these days till you have to buy it, and then it's worth its weight in gold. And I should imagine Dacre's hours are as heavy as tombstones."

I didn't tell him that Catherine was footing the bill; probably he guessed from my casual reply that it wasn't the fees that were troubling me. He made no comment; I daresay, considering the peculiar circumstances of the case, he didn't think it strange.

So I told him of my failure. "I was counting on him," I wound up. "It's a horrible blow."

"Herringham's the best barrister in England," Bannister agreed. "I suppose he wanted a small fortune?"

"Wouldn't touch it," I repeated gloomily.

"Too busy? At this time of year?" Bannister was incredulous.

"Nothing so simple. He believes Dacre's guilty, and refuses to soil his hands with the case. He's suggested a fellow called Wareing—Charteris Wareing. I don't know the man myself except by repute. But I believe he's a very straight man."

"He's all right," Bannister reassured me. "Curiously enough, I was dining with the fellow a day or two ago, and we discussed the case. Well, naturally. He's extremely interested. It isn't as if it were a common or garden murder; Chandos was a well-known man, and the peculiar circumstances have given the whole affair a tremendous publicity. I should think he'd take it on like a shot if you offer it to him. Forlorn hopes are what he likes; he's the K.C. who pulled young Lancing through when they'd practically erected the gallows for him. Of course, his fee would be pretty steep, though he might shade it a bit, since Dacre's a poor man."

"The fee will be all right," I said again, a trifle testily. "Dacre may be penniless, but he isn't quite friendless yet."

"Of course not," Bannister agreed, and then paused again. He was clearly embarrassed, struggling against a possible infringement of good taste.

"Ravenswood," he broke out suddenly, "has it occurred to you that possibly Lady Chandos herself isn't sure of Dacre's innocence?"

"Several times. But of course she'll stick by him now."

"She will. She's reached the stage where she doesn't really care if he's guilty or not. Believe me, I know what I'm saying. I've dabbled a bit in psychology, and all Lady Chandos wants now is the fellow for her own property. His ethical or moral qualities don't appeal to her, except as they affect her. Do you know what I mean? The fact that Dacre may have murdered her husband is more or less wiped out by the fact that he did it because his need of her was so tremendous that he was willing to take even that mighty risk for her sake. And because of that she'll perjure herself without hesitation to save him; but if she were to discover that he was playing her false, had been unfaithful to her and was interested in another woman, then she'd forget her own interests, and she'd go into the witness-box and swear her own life away, if necessary, to get her revenge. As far as reason goes women have not progressed much from the stage of the savage whose head can hold only one idea at a time. That's where men score. They do, as a rule, take the impersonal standpoint; women see life as individuals, and it's as individuals that they regulate their lives. Law-givers? No sane man wants to see laws made by women. To begin with, not one in ten has a grain of respect for the law she wants to create. Lady Chandos hasn't; Miss Dennis hasn't. As for Miss St Claire, I don't suppose she cares either. By the way," he coloured, aware of less than normal tact in his manner of bringing the conversation round to her, "she's in town, I hear. Is she with Lady Chandos?"

His tone, which he strove to make impersonal, implied how great was his dislike of the idea of her being cooped up with Catherine. He betrayed then his secret apprehension that she had been in some way a party to her husband's murder, an attitude of mind that shocked and dismayed me.

"She's in London certainly," I agreed. "Staying with a woman she knows. I can give you her address if you'd like it."

He hesitated, then shook his head. "Kind of you, but I'm afraid it wouldn't be any use. She's very young and at twenty one 'swings the earth, a trinket, at the wrist.' As soon as this affair has ceased to be a nine days' wonder I expect to see the announcement. In the meantime, I don't want to make things worse for her. She took Chandos' death pretty hard. Coming back to Wareing—would you care to meet him, quite without prejudice? Talk to him, you understand, and see how he feels, and what you think of the idea? It can be quite a social meeting. Dinner at my flat—shall we say tomorrow?"

I closed with the suggestion gladly enough. I felt responsible to Catherine, and I was grateful to Bannister for his offer. I knew Wareing's record; he was one of the finest men of his profession —loyal, honourable, keenly sensitive to the dignity of his calling, a magnificent pleader, an indefatigable worker. We should be fortunate to get him.

His reputation was so considerable that the smallness of the man himself came as something of a shock. He wasn't above five feet five, a thin, dark, wiry man, looking about two-and-forty, though he was actually some years older, with thin, dark hair, an olive complexion, a dominant nose, and a manner that inspired confidence and respect.

"I'm interested in the case," he confessed, "psychologically it's extraordinarily attractive. I may as well admit that the individual who takes my interest from the outset is Miss Dennis. She's a well-known type, the woman who's suffered from sexual repression from childhood, who's sternly crushed all natural desires, and has grown up like a tree planted under an overhanging cliff, robust but warped. She's got personality, more personality, if I may say so, than either of the central figures. She and Sir Simon occupy all the foreground; the rest are simply a setting for them. And as he fades out of the picture it really leaves her in the limelight."

We discussed the case in greater detail during dinner and afterwards when the cigars went round. He didn't smoke himself, and drank very little. Towards the end of the evening I offered him the case on his own terms. He accepted it immediately.

"It shouldn't be a particularly expensive affair, as far as investigation goes," he said, "but we have to formulate a theory that will acquit Dacre beyond all doubt."

"We haven't got to prove his innocence," Bannister demurred.

"The Crown have got to prove his guilt. All we have to do is to rake up enough doubt to get him an acquittal."

Wareing's eyes burned like smoky fires. "I beg your pardon. That sort of game may be well enough for some men, but not for me. Either Captain Dacre is innocent or he is not. If he is, I should be guilty of negligence if I left a stone unturned to force that fact home on the minds of the public. If he is not, I shall have no option but to resign the case. But—psychologically again—I feel certain that he is not guilty."

"And how do we set about proving it?"

"There's only one way, and that is by showing beyond question that some one else did it."

"Is it possible?"

"If he didn't, some one must have done." He considered for a few moments. "I think we have only one chance," he began again, "and that is to prove that he is the victim of a carefully-planned, hideously-unscrupulous plot to cast the blame on him. The mass of evidence against him seems to justify such a suspicion. Now, there is one feature of the case on which no one has so far commented, or at any rate not publicly, and that is that the foundation-stone of the case against him is Miss Dennis' evidence. She swears she heard him limping downstairs at one in the morning. Now, it is noteworthy that no one else has corroborated her evidence and yet it is on her word that the whole of the rest of the case against him has been built up. Captain Dacre's room is on the same floor as Egerton's, yours," he nodded to me, "and Bannister's. Evidence shows that you had not separated above half an hour, when he is alleged to have gone downstairs, making sufficient noise to rouse Miss Dennis, but not enough to waken any one else. It is not even as though Captain Dacre's room were the one at the head of the stairs, for, according to the rough plan Bannister has drawn up for me, his is the last room of the four. Miss St Claire, who testified to hearing him go up to bed at midnight, sleeps next to Miss Dennis, but she heard nothing. That, of course, is less strange, since she might well fall asleep within the hour, and if she is a deep sleeper the sound would be insufficient to wake her. Following up that suggestion, it is curious to see that practically all the remaining evidence against Dacre springs from Miss Dennis. It is she who speaks of the letter Chandos sent him, asking him not to come to Freyne; she who accuses Lady Chandos of neglecting and unfairly treating her husband; certainly it is she who is largely responsible for the general attitude towards the dead man's wife. When suicide was mooted, she said wildly that he had been driven to it by her; when it was definitely established as a carefully-calculated murder, she practically arraigned Lady Chandos and her lover as his murderers. She had in her possession the mortgage on Dacre Court—or, at least, the knowledge of its existence; she was in Sir Simon's confidence as to his incurable disease and the tablets he took to allay the pain. She was alone for twenty minutes in the library on the evening before the crime; she could write the bogus third letter then, blotting it in Chandos' pad. In fact, she had all the materials to her hand for a perfect plot. Now let us, for a moment, assume that she is the guilty party. No doubt her original thought was to suggest suicide. But, if that failed (and in the excitement of the moment the most practised criminal frequently makes a fatal slip, as she did by placing the pen in the right hand), then it was to appear that Dacre was guilty. She had her story perfectly prepared. She had heard a step in the night; Dacre needed money; his host had written to him asking him to stay away; Lady Chandos had written equally urgently asking him to come down. There was a third letter, whose authenticity has not yet been proved, threatening to dispossess him of the house he loved unless he complied with Chandos' wishes. Whether she knew that Dacre was on the high-road to becoming a morpho-maniac, I don't yet know, but if she did, there was her case complete. Of course, Lady Chandos almost ruined the scheme by her swift, instinctive defence of Dacre. (I should say, in parenthesis, that she isn't quite sure herself of her lover's innocence.) Whether her story is true or not it is impossible for us to guess at present. It's quite possible.

"Then there is the matter of the will. I understand that Miss Dennis has sworn she knew nothing of its contents. There, again, we have only her own testimony. But suppose our theory is right. She hears Ravenswood come upstairs and shut his door, waits a little to make certain that the coast is clear, and seizes her opportunity. Of all the people in the house she is the one of whom no awkward questions will be asked. She is taking down the notes of the *Quarterly Art Review* manuscript at which she has been working late, as there is some urgency about the matter. Possibly, she did actually take it with her, carefully bringing it back again later so as to avoid all awkward clues that might point to her presence in the room after dinner. She had unique opportunities for studying and copying the writing both of Sir Simon and of Captain Dacre. She has access to his blotting-book; I am inclined to believe that letter was forged. It was very uncharacteristic of Chandos to stoop to threats. As for the seal, that was probably a happy chance. Dacre must have dropped it earlier in the evening, and she, finding it, kept it as additional evidence of his guilt. She may either have left it in the room at the time of the murder, or she may have kept it until the morning of the 23rd, waiting to see which way the cat would jump. I am inclined to think the latter. Then, when she saw that it was to be not suicide but murder, she dropped the seal unostentatiously on the floor and went away with the others, leaving a trail of damning evidence against an innocent man.

"Next comes the question of the tablets. She alone, of all the people in the house, knew that Chandos was taking them; she knew, on her own showing, where they were kept; she knew, therefore, that if he were found poisoned, seemingly by his own hand, there must be reasonable evidence that he had access to such means of self-destruction. It was, she argued, a hundred to one chance that either Bradlaugh or Frobisher should realise the stuff had been injected. Moreover, no one knew exactly how many tablets Chandos had taken, so she simply had to extract the requisite number to make up the amount of the morphia and conceal them. She never dreamed that the fragments of white dust that she scattered so casually behind the brass tray would be reassembled and brought as evidence against her. Now, the chief thing is to find a motive."

"The money," hazarded Bannister.

"The money, by all means. Still, we shall have to produce something more definite than that vague suspicion on which to build a case. Our trouble at the moment is that we know nothing of Miss Dennis beyond the fact that she was Chandos' secretary for five years. There may be any number of dark secrets in her past; on the other hand, there may be nothing but a blameless stretch of—what is it?—five-and-thirty years. But supposing that there is something and that she is being blackmailed? She daren't take the risk of exposing the blackmailer—not one woman in a hundred has the courage—so she has to get hold of the money somehow. I don't know what Chandos paid her, but even if it was generous—and it probably was—it wouldn't be much use in fending off a blackguard. Then there is only one way, and that is somehow to lay hands on the five thousand pounds. It is another nail in her coffin that, though she might have pulled off the scheme with even better effect within one or two nights of Chandos' return from London (for men are far more likely to give up the ghost when the shock of bad news is still on them) she waits until the new will has been drawn up. I grant you she was clever—so clever that if we aren't careful, she may elude us yet. She chose a time when Chandos was deeply hurt; in a flash she saw her opportunity and took it. Here is the best excuse for suicide that has come her way. Every one will naturally blame Lady Chandos; no shadow of suspicion will ever attach to her. So she lays her plans. As I have already suggested, she creeps noiselessly out of her room, down to the library, gets admission without arousing any doubts in Chandos' mind, accomplishes her end, and the rest is plain sailing. She has already prepared the crumpled sheets in her own room, and has brought them with her. For all we know she has been laying plans ever since the drawing up of the second will. Chandos, Dacre, Lady Chandos, all play into her hands. But who has ever thought of Althea Dennis as a personality at all? She was one of the servants, like one of the pieces of furniture with a name to distinguish it from all the rest. Lady Chandos was doubtless courteous to her on all occasions, but she is not the type that fraternises with employees. Nor would it occur to her to be jealous of any of them. Then came Miss Dennis' supreme burst of genius. When the body is found she turns on the dead man's wife, and upbraids her for cruelty, crying aloud the bitter story of her own unrequited love. That deceived you all. It also served to divert any breath of suspicion that might have blown in her direction. When she discovers her one blunder, she fiercely accuses Lady Chandos and Dacre of wilful murder. But she is too clever to lay her cards on the table an instant before she need. No doubt the story of the footstep was in her mind long before the arrival of the police. But she did not intend to give the pair an opportunity of escape from the net she had woven for them."

"And what's our first step?" asked Bannister, after a time.

"I must get a man to hunt out Miss Dennis' antecedents, discover what she did or was before she came to Freyne; whether she has relations; whether there is any one in her life with a sinister hold upon her. I think I'll get Stuart on the job. He's the best man I know; expensive, but I gather your friend is indifferent as to that."

"We want the best people," I agreed.

"Exactly. Blackmail, I confess, is the only thing that will support our claim. Unless we can prove that, our case falls to the ground. But Stuart will get the truth if any man can."

"I wouldn't have his job for a thousand guineas," said Bannister frankly. "Tackling a woman like that.... How on earth does he set about it? He can't very well hunt her out and put the brutal question to her."

"If that were all we wanted I could get a journalist at five pounds a week," said Wareing dryly. "This is work that needs great delicacy of touch. That's why I selected Stuart. He knows the rules of the game."

I felt as curious as Bannister. "How will he tackle it?" I asked.

Wareing's thin dark brows lifted expressively. "That's what he's paid to discover. We don't map out his course for him. I think you'll find he'll be quite satisfactory."

"I don't know if Lady Chandos could help," I suggested suddenly. "She might know where Chandos heard of her, some story of her past. I can't say."

"No," returned Wareing energetically, "Lady Chandos must emphatically not be approached. In fact the question of Miss Dennis being under suspicion must not be mentioned to her. It wouldn't be fair."

"To whom?" queried Bannister grimly.

"To me—or to her—or to Miss Dennis. Lady Chandos' chief aim at the moment is to secure Captain Dacre's release. If she thinks there is a chance of Miss Dennis being put in his shoes, she'll work tooth and nail to convict her. Purely coincidental details that we, seeing the matter 'off,' as it were, would regard dispassionately, would assume tremendous proportions to her. I am, of course, undertaking the case on Captain Dacre's behalf, but we must be careful not to tilt the scales of justice. I have your assurance that nothing of our suspicions will be passed on to Lady Chandos, unless and until we have reached the stage where it will be necessary for us to take the rest of the world into our confidence?"

We agreed, of course, and soon after the party broke up. Wareing and I walked part of the way together. As he talked I was reminded suddenly of Lidgett, a great chess-player of the 90's, whom I was taken to see as a child. Just so did the lawyer stoop over an enormous chess-board moving the pieces this way and that. Already I had ceased to be a human being in his eyes. I was just a pawn on his momentous board.

It was not a nice sensation.

II

The next morning I went to see Catherine, to tell her of the plans I had made. She wrinkled her forehead. "Wareing? Wareing? Oh, yes, I believe I have heard the name. But what was wrong with the other one? Simon used to know him. I should have liked to feel he had taken it on."

"He couldn't do it," I said uncomfortably.

"Why? You explained to him, surely, that he could name his own fee?"

"It was nothing to do with fees."

"Then what?"

"He, like Wareing, regards his profession as a sacred trust. And his feelings wouldn't let him defend Dacre."

Catherine whitened. "You mean, he thinks——"

"He thinks the charge well-founded. Wareing, on the other hand—and believe me, his reputation is nearly as considerable as Herringham's—is equally certain Dacre is innocent. That's half the battle."

"It isn't what he believes that matters, but what he makes the judge and jury believe."

"If any one can save Dacre he'll do it."

"He's *got* to save him," she cried fiercely. "You know, don't you, that he's innocent? You believe it? Say you believe it."

She spoke with extraordinary passion, unaware, poor soul, that she was betraying herself with every inflection. Her knowledge of Wareing's integrity set up a new terror, lest during the progress of the case he should become convinced of his client's guilt and abandon the whole thing.

Now, in reply to Catherine's question I said candidly, "I don't know. There's a state of mind—Dacre's state is so abnormal..."

"You think I've lied to shield my husband's murderer? Thrown away my good name for a whim?"

I felt awkward. Then I said in my ungainly fashion that we all knew what she had done for his sake, and admired her courage. As to Dacre, I was quite honest. I wasn't absolutely sure, and said so.

Catherine's eyes hardened. "You, too! Poor Rupert! He's almost bankrupt now the balance has weighed against him."

"As long as he has you, he won't much care for the rest of the world," I told her.

She laughed bitterly. "It's the rest of the world who will judge him," she cried. "I can't be much use to him. Oh, all right, Alan. I leave everything to you. It's good of you to take so much trouble, feeling as you do."

CHAPTER 8 THE ANONYMOUS LETTER

I give Stuart's story as, later, he told it to us.

Like Wareing, he realised that the most important point was to discover something of the inner circumstances of Althea Dennis' life; and it seemed to him that his best chance was to get her in a position where he would have a right to put certain intimate questions and she, without intimidation, to answer them—that is, the right of prospective employer and employed. It was a moot point whether, in all the circumstances, she would be seeking another post, but it was the best suggestion his imagination could offer. And so, two mornings later, there appeared in the *Times* and the *Telegraph* this advertisement:—

"ARTIST—living in the country, requires resident secretary (lady). Not under 30. Preferably with similar experience. First-class shorthand and typewriting essential. Good salary to efficient worker. Apply with details of age, experience and qualifications (copies of testimonials only) to Box X. IIIII., The *Times*, E.C., 4.

Then he engaged a small service flat near Bloomsbury, and waited for results. The replies were overwhelming. Every type of woman in the country seemed anxious to become private secretary to an unknown artist. But the only thing Stuart wanted, which was the signature of Althea Dennis, never came. Of course, his position was no worse than he had anticipated.

Very probably she would not, so soon after the tragedy, be seeking work at all. In any case, her connection with the Chandos affair would militate against her interests. No doubt there were other people in the world who had solved the problem after the manner of Charteris Wareing.

Of course, we had her address in London; Bradlaugh had obtained hers with every one else's before we left Freyne. But that was very little use to him. To accost a perfectly strange woman, and a rather dangerous one at that, without any excuse, was hopeless, and would merely have aroused her suspicions. When it became clear that his advertisement was sterile, Stuart next began the round of the employment offices. At each he said, "Is there any one on your books at the moment whom you could specially recommend?" in the hope that one day one would reply, "There's Miss Dennis; she might suit you." But no one ever did.

He decided at last to abandon the frail hope and to go down to the rooms where Miss Dennis was living. Effectually disguised he might ask for lodgings there, and either scrape up some sort of acquaintance with the woman herself, or, far more likely, draw the landlady into conversation. He knew from experience that such people are frequently garrulous, particularly if they scent anything in the nature of a mystery. He had secured the evidence for the arrest of Mme. de Caux, the celebrated French murderess, by these means. But before he was driven to that rather dangerous expedient something happened that turned the scales in our favour. I met Catherine in Bond Street.

She was walking alone, despondent, and (I thought) a little nervous. When she saw me she said quickly, "Unless you're afraid of your reputation being blasted by merely being seen with me, offer me some tea, Alan. Anywhere you like."

I took her to Rumpelmayers. And over tea she talked. She was in an apprehensive and unstable frame of mind; thin and very colourless I thought her, and her quick impatience and consequent air of apology struck me oddly. It was the more noticeable because of her amazing self-control hitherto. Either something new had occurred to disturb her, or her fears (and doubts) on Dacre's behalf were tormenting her more keenly than ever.

"Talk to me as if I were an ordinary human being," she said suddenly. "I feel like the leper of old. Wherever I go I ring my bell, and cry 'Unclean! Unclean!' What's happened to every one? Is there any news of an engagement between Rosemary... and young Egerton yet, or is that another life I've spoiled? It won't be a nice thing for him, all this publicity. So far he's only touched by the fringe of its mantle, but if he marries Rosemary every one will recall that they were staying together in the house of a notorious woman, and that may damage his career. A politician, when he's rising, has to be as blameless as a woman before she achieves a wedding-ring." She laughed, as if she had said something exceedingly humorous, but it didn't ring true. It was not worthy of Catherine.

I told her I had heard nothing, but that I was certain Egerton's decorum would not allow him to announce an engagement while uncertainty still hung over the death of Simon Chandos. He had attended the funeral with a crape band on his arm, and he would wear it mentally until the matter had been cleared up.

"He was rather deeply attached to Chandos, wasn't he?" I added.

Catherine's brow darkened a little. "He'd every reason to be," she said dryly. "But don't let's talk about him. I hope you're right though. I don't want Rosemary's life broken up by a cruel streak of bad luck. She adores the boy—though for myself I confess he's a little too inhuman. Like a perfectly-modelled machine, and she's so volatile. I only pray if it does come to anything that she won't allow him to compress her gradually into one of those pale expressionless wives who so often seem to be tacked on to successful politicians. He's so very circumspect—now!"

"Now?" I repeated softly, but Catherine did not take the hint.

"And the rest?" she went on, "I suppose you don't see anything of young Egerton or that rather nice Bannister man Rosemary brought down to Freyne. A trifle crude, that, even for Rosemary."

"As a matter of fact, I have seen Bannister. He introduced me to Wareing."

"I'm rather sorry for him," Catherine went on thoughtfully. "He's in a hopeless position, and he's too fine a man to be tossed aside for a young girl's experience."

"I don't think Rosemary's that sort," I expostulated.

"Oh, she won't mean it, but she's at the age when the attentions of a middle-aged man are rather amusing. The very young can't realise that people double their years still have hearts that can be broken. Rosemary won't take him seriously. No girl of twenty, in love with a youngster not much older, would. He probably seems preposterous to her. And I suppose Althea Dennis has gone back to her ridiculous Horne creature."

"Who," I asked casually, "is the Horne creature?"

"Some absurd old woman who keeps a dark, old-fashioned little registry office, where no one new ever goes, and where all the old ones die because they've no more life left in them. Simon got her from there, and she used to talk, when she first came, of this Miss Horne—how safe she was, how careful, how one could always rely on her. But if she hasn't got the *nous* to try somewhere more modern, I don't suppose she stands much chance of getting a good post."

"She hasn't applied to you for a character, has she?" I asked.

"No," returned Catherine, her face hardening, "and I hope, for her own sake, she won't. She's done her best to ruin mine. Oh, don't look disapproving, Alan. I'm not a saint in a glass window. Besides, she's too much sense for that. I don't suppose people will be anxious to have a secretary so much in the public eye as she is, and is bound to be when the case actually comes off." Then she made another of her restless gestures. "Oh, we won't talk about her," she cried. "She can be trusted to guard her own interests. Anyway, why should I care? There's something worse still to be faced. It's driving me mad."

She glanced round hastily as she spoke; her raised voice had attracted a little attention from the occupants of tables close by, and she talked hurriedly of commonplace things until their minds were distracted again. Then she opened her bag, a handsome crocodile affair Chandos had given her, and handed me a square white envelope, made of cheap paper, containing a single sheet with a few words written in a straight characterless script.

"If you are interested in the return of your letter to your lover of the 8th July, communicate with Box 002, *Morning Standard*."

"Now," said Catherine, as I set the sheet down, "you realise why my nerves are torn to rags. Oh, it's very sweet of you, Alan, to pretend to notice nothing, but I'm not quite a fool. I'm nearly crazy with terror. This threat—on top of everything else."

"You know the letter referred to."

"Yes. I couldn't easily forget it."

"Ah! Is there anything in it so critical that you'd scruple to put the matter into the hands of the police?"

Catherine stared in horrified amazement. "Alan! Are you mad? A letter I wrote to Rupert. . . . I was almost delirious when I sent it to him—and you'd have it starred in the *News of the World*!"

I felt slightly abashed. "I only thought, seeing that it's impossible to hush up the story of—of you and Dacre, at this stage, it might be wiser for you to grasp your nettle boldly, and show up whoever it is to the authorities."

She regarded me steadfastly for a time. Then she said, in a still, incredulous voice, "Do you know what you're suggesting? Have you ever seen an underground spring in the place where it suddenly bubbles up out of the ground? It's like a geyser, isn't it? That's how it was with me. I'd been running underground for three years; I'd done my level best to run a smooth, correct course; and then it was no use, I had to come up, and I took the lid off my feelings, and they shot upwards. It makes me hot even now to think of some of the things in that letter. And all you can suggest is that I should hand the matter over to the police!"

"It isn't only yourself," I blundered. "It's all the other people he's got in his net. The successful blackmailer doesn't depend on one man or one woman for a livelihood."

Catherine was still watching me in that fixed, frozen way,

"What do you think I am?" she asked. "If that letter falls into the hands of the police it may seal Rupert's sentence. It was a wild piece of folly—but I loved him so, and I didn't stop to think it might come to this. I'd forgotten how careless he is. He must have left it about, and it's fallen into the hands of some vile person who realises that I'm a rich woman who'd spend a good deal of money to keep the matter quiet."

"Have you any suspicions?" I asked, a sudden thought striking through my mind that her supposition might be correct, and that the blackmailer might actually be one of the men employed by Dacre. True, Philpott had spoken of a woman in black, but she might be simply their agent. It wouldn't be possible for one of them to get away with such a scheme. The more I thought of it the more likely did it seem that here was the explanation.

"What is it?" demanded Catherine excitedly. "You've thought of something—I can see it in your face. Have you any idea who it might be?"

I said reluctantly, "I was wondering whether you were right. Perhaps it's only fair for you to know that Chandos was being blackmailed in much the same way, by some unknown woman shortly before his death."

Catherine's eyes dilated; the rest of her face became shrunken and pinched; the dark smudges under her eyes stood out in relief against the ashen whiteness of her skin.

"Then he knew? And he never said a word. I wouldn't have asked Rupert to come down if I'd guessed. Any other man but Simon would have spoken of it, beaten me, disgraced me before all men. But he just bore that, as he bore everything else—disappointment and disillusion and fatal illness and agony—without a complaint. And this woman got hold of him?"

"She swore to him that the letter he bought was the only one she had."

"Perhaps at the time that was true. When was this?"

I recollected. "Oh, before you ever wrote this second letter."

"Alan, I think it must be one of Rupert's servants. Some one who systematically stole the letters as they came in, and passed them on to an accomplice."

"If you'll give it to me," I said, "I'll pass it on to a private detective Dacre's lawyer is employing, and he'll discover the author. You shall have it back somehow."

Still she hesitated. "Promise me one thing," she said at last, laying her ungloved hand on mine. Hers was burning hot. Indeed her whole aspect was feverish. "I'd sooner pay all the money I've got than let Scotland Yard get hold of that letter for the benefit of the public. I suppose you think I'm idiotic now that every one knows the story. But even they don't know everything. There's so little of our lives that can be kept sacred. Don't try and take from me the fragments that remain."

I felt a bit doubtful about that. If the letter should prove to be an important factor in the case against Chandos' murderer it was almost bound to come into court. I tried to make Catherine see that.

"In any case," I urged, "you're no worse off by letting me do what I can. If you refuse, you're more likely to give the game away by inexperience. And I'll strain every nerve to get you back your letter untampered with."

We compromised on that, and she gave me the letter. That evening I rang up Wareing, told him about Miss Horne, and said that I would come in person next morning with the anonymous script, whose postmark was the undistinguished one of Ludgate Circus.

CHAPTER 9 THE MAN OF MYSTERY

I

The next morning Stuart continued his search after Miss Dennis. The telephone book yielded him Miss Horne's address, and after a little trouble he found the place—a tiny, dark office up several flights of stairs in a house just off St George's Square.

"I am an artist," he began, presenting a card inscribed "James Parkinson," and the address of the temporary flat, "and I want to engage a resident secretary. I was recommended to come to you...."

"By whom?" snapped Miss Horne.

"My late hostess was one of your clients many years ago," Stuart improvised hastily. "She was a Miss Robinson."

"There have been a good many Robinsons on my books," Miss Horne agreed disappointedly. "Yes?"

Stuart described in some detail the sort of woman he wanted. He added that he was married, and was contemplating buying a house at Dovercourt, Hampshire.

"I am particularly anxious to get some one who has previously done similar work," he wound up.

Miss Horne considered for a few moments. Then she rapped out, "I know some one who would suit you admirably. She has been secretary to an English artist for the past five years. Her references are excellent, and she would not be leaving him now but for his unexpected death."

Stuart, his pulses rising with hope, murmured decorously, "Yes. . . . ?"

"I feel sure she would suit you," Miss Horne went on, "there is only the question. You have, of course, heard of Sir Simon Chandos' tragic and mysterious death."

"The fact of his death is enough for me. I don't read the newspaper details. Is this lady concerned in it?"

"She was his secretary, and she has come in for a certain amount of most undesirable notoriety. She is, in fact, the chief witness in the case, and it is her evidence that has brought the criminal to book. But, as you will realise, that is rather against her in her search for employment. Prospective employers hesitate. . . . Very ridiculous, no doubt, but there it is."

"Dovercourt is a small place and very quiet," Stuart reassured her. "I doubt if the death of Sir Simon Chandos will be much discussed. I don't think Miss—did you tell me her name?—would find herself the subject of much unwelcome publicity."

"It is not that so much as your personal point of view. What time would it be convenient for Miss Dennis to call?"

"I shall be in all this afternoon," said Stuart, and went away.

Althea Dennis turned up soon after lunch. She was dressed entirely in black, an extravaganza of mourning for Simon Chandos—long black skirt, black poplin blouse, black straw hat with a dejected black ribbon bow, heavy black shoes, black woollen stockings, and black kid gloves. She was a trifle flat-footed, and moved without any kind of spring or lightness. Her face was very pale and puffed-looking, the face of a woman who has known much mental strain.

Stuart greeted her and talked for some time on purely formal aspects of her work. Then he said, "There is another point. I want to make arrangements that I may regard as permanent—for two or three years, at all events. You are not likely to be forced, perhaps through the illness or death of a relative, to throw up your work at short notice?"

"I have no relatives," said Althea Dennis sombrely.

"And—if you will pardon the question—you are not engaged

to be married?"

"No, I am not. There is no one who has any claims on me. I am as keen as you seem to be to come to some lasting arrangement. I have my living to earn, and nothing but my savings to fall back on at such times as these."

I don't suppose Stuart felt he was getting much forrader. But he asked for her testimonials, in the hope that he might thus discover a little more about her. But the effort was fruitless. Miss Dennis had brought with her two references, one from a Mrs Carrick, with whom she had lived for three years before taking up work with Chandos and the other from a Lady Rose, now dead. So that didn't help Stuart much either, particularly as it transpired that Mrs Carrick had since married a missionary, and had gone to spread the Word in the wilds of Africa.

"I can't tell you quite definitely for a day or two," he summed up at last, "I have two or three other applicants to see. You are free now?"

"Yes. I will leave you my telephone number. You understand," she hesitated, "if you are thinking of applying to Lady Chandos for a reference, there may be some difficulty. I am the chief witness in the case against Captain Dacre."

"And that prejudices you in her eyes? I haven't, as I say, read the details."

"He was her lover," said Miss Dennis with suppressed rage.

"In that case, I quite see it would be useless to attempt to secure her recommendation," observed Stuart dryly.

But after she had gone, he thought ruefully that of all he had hoped to learn he had discovered very little. That she had no relations—but did that help him? If she needed money urgently probably it would not be for a relative at all. And he did not see how, as matters stood at present, he was ever to learn the hidden motive that might have actuated her. Nor, during the next two days, did he learn anything fresh. At the end of forty-eight hours he took the bull by the horns and went round to the house where she lodged. Just opposite was a tall, dilapidated building, in whose basement a mediocre tea-room had been opened. From the window it was possible to watch the front and area doors of No. 29. Stuart drank strong tea and ploughed resolutely through stale bread-and-butter till the door opened and Miss Dennis came down the steps. The afternoon sky was clear, but there was a hint of rain in the wind; he noticed that she carried both mackintosh and umbrella.

"Doesn't expect to be back till late," he reasoned, and watched her board an omnibus. For a further five minutes he lingered in case she returned, then went across to No. 29 and pulled the bell. The landlady, a short stout woman in a blue dress, decorated with fat white goldfish, greeted him civilly enough until he asked for Miss Dennis. Then her manner changed, becoming menacing.

"Are you another of 'em?" she demanded fiercely.

"Another?" Stuart retreated a step.

"Yes, that's what I said. Because if you are, let me tell you, this is a respectable house. 'Ave you got a message to leave?"

"I'm afraid there's some misunderstanding. Miss Dennis called on me the other day with reference to a position as residential secretary, but I told her I could not altogether make up my mind at the moment. However, I have decided now, and as I was passing her house thought I might call in and see her for a moment and settle things in person. So much more satisfactory than a letter."

The landlady seemed a trifle mollified. "Oh well, if that's what you want, it's all right, I'm sorry if I spoke 'asty, I'm sure. And I ain't got nothink against Miss Dennis, except that way she 'as of talking to 'erself when there ain't no one there. I thought p'raps you was like the other one."

"Another gentleman who wanted a secretary?"

"Not 'im. I know what 'e wanted. Great big bolsheviki man, with a black beard and black moustaches and gert black eyebrows. Asks if Miss Dennis is in and when I tells 'im 'No,' asks me if there's a message for him, a letter p'raps what she's left in her room. Wouldn't leave no name, though. Jest looks dark and wicked and says, 'Tell 'er the time grows short. I will come tomorrow.' Well, Miss Dennis *says* she don't know 'oo 'e is, but she stays in next day all the same. Never stirs out not so far as the post."

"And did she see him when he did come?" murmured Stuart with well-feigned indifference.

"'E never come. Miss Dennis, she says she won't stay in for 'im no more, and next day out she goes. And sure enough, she ain't been gone more'n arf an hour when 'e turns up again. 'Is Miss Dennis in today?' 'e asks. 'No, she ain't,' I tells him, 'why didn't you come yesterday like you said?' 'Did she expect me yesterday?' I tells 'im Miss Dennis don't even know 'oo 'e is. 'She knows me all right,' 'e answers quiet-like, 'no message?' 'None,' I says, shutting the door. And then 'e begins to nod 'is 'ead up and down like a great doll, 'is big wicked brown face, and 'is big black beard, and 'is eyebrows and moustaches all keeping time. 'Tell 'er,' 'e says, 'there's only three days more and then it'll be too late.' And orf 'e marches."

"What did Miss Dennis say when you told her?"

"She was all put out; went on somethink awful. Turns on me desprit-like and flings up 'er 'ands and cries out, ''Ow can I 'elp it if they pesters me? Oh, God, if I could 'ave a little peace. But I ain't 'ad no peace since 'e died.'"

"How long ago was that?"

"Yesterday. 'E's due to come the day arter tomorrow, and then I'll find out somethink, as sure as me name's Kate Garland."

"Have you no idea what he wants?"

"Money, 'o course. That sort usually does. 'E's bleeding 'er white, if you ask me, sir. No wonder she wants a job. You get 'er away from 'ere, if you can, away from that man."

"I feel a little perturbed," Stuart confessed. "Indeed, I should be obliged if you wouldn't mention my visit here. Since I've heard about this man I feel inclined to alter my mind. Suppose he followed her down to my house! My wife would be terrified out of her wits. She isn't very strong."

"Bless you, sir, I understands," said Mrs Garland maternally. "I bin through it more times than I can count. No, you can take it from me what this vagabone wants is money. 'E's got some 'old over 'er. What did she mean about the one what died and 'er 'aving no peace?"

"Did you say he was shabbily-dressed?"

"Not 'im, only odd. A big black cloak affair, and a black hat with a broad brim, and a deep, funny voice, and this beard and all. Oh, and 'e said last time, 'I warned 'er! I warned 'er!'"

"I suppose he didn't give you a name?"

"No, 'e didn't, but the day after 'e come the last time 'e sent 'er a letter, not signed nor nothink, but jest written on a bit of paper. I found it afterwards in 'er basket—not tore up nor nothink. 'Friday is the last day.' And still she says "E must be mad! 'E must be mad!'"

"I should think that's the answer," Stuart approved. "I suppose you didn't think to keep the letter?"

Mrs Garland bridled indignantly. "No, sir, I did not keep the letter, such not being my 'abit wiv letters addressed to persons not myself."

"I was only thinking that if this man is a dangerous character it might help in locating him," Stuart explained soothingly. "Indeed, as Miss Dennis has repeatedly said, she doesn't know who he is, it looks as though that must be the answer to the riddle."

"If you could 'ear 'er talking, and talking to 'erself, sir, night after night, and sometimes in the early morning too, you'd not feel so easy in your mind. She's got something on 'er soul that's 'arf-killing 'er, and I'm as sure as my name's Kate Garland that it's something to do with that man."

II

Stuart came away from the house thoughtful, and a little elated. He had learned what we all wanted to know, that there was a secret in Althea Dennis' life that might well provide a motive for murder. He was inclined to agree with Mrs Garland that money was the man's objective. It next remained for him to learn the nature of her secret. Was it possible that her uncompromising exterior masked some guilty passion, whose revelation she so greatly feared that she preferred to take the risk of death? Or were they merely partners? Hardly that, or he would not come to her house with threats. Perhaps he was aware of her guilt in the Chandos' case and was blackmailing her to her last penny.

After some deliberation it seemed to him that his best chance was to be in the same house at the time of the strange man's call, so the following afternoon he disguised himself as a clerk (toothbrush moustache, light brown hair *en brosse*, pince-nez, the deplorable round jacket and striped trousers that a slavish generation has retained when it discarded many finer habits of its forbears, bright yellow gloves, bright brown boots, a bowler-hat, a pasty complexion and snub nose, obtained by a little expert manipulation) and called at No. 29, where the familiar card "APARTMENTS" was to be seen in the ground-floor front window.

Mrs Garland greeted him with approval. "Rooms? Oh, bless you, yes! She had rooms. One lovely one now, on the second floor, looking over the street, as nice a room as you could want. And just vacant. Would the gentleman come up and see?" The gentleman would. She calculated with the eye of an expert, as she led the way, the value of the prospective lodger's clothes, knew to a penny what he had paid for the shirt, the shoes and the hat. The suit she liked; it was quiet and superior-looking; some of the young men who had come here looked as if they'd stripped a peg for half-a-sovereign. Possibly they had. A clerk, she decided, and a young one. She preferred them young. Experience had taught her that clerks over forty were usually journalists out of a job, and they didn't hold their clerical ones long. After about a month they were drifting about the streets looking for something to do, and at the end of the week that meant she was looking for her rent.

"This is the room, sir," she said. It was a pleasant room, a little stuffy because the window had not been opened for a week; open windows mean dust, and a grass-widow who lets out rooms has little enough to spare for servants' wages. "Would you want your meals in?"

"Breakfast, of course—and mostly a meal at night. I shall be out all day."

"That's right, sir. Dinner, of course? Most of my young gents has dinner. Chop and pertaters? That's right. I'm sure you'll be most comfortable, sir." And she began to discuss terms.

Stuart deliberately prolonged the conversation. He was listening for a sound from the room above. Suddenly it came, a steady, regular noise, like some small solid article being bumped on the floor.

"What's that?" demanded Stuart. "Sounds like a sewing-machine. I'm leaving my present rooms because I can't stand the sewing-machine the woman overhead treadles every night. It gives me a headache; besides, I have to study."

"She 'asn't got no sewing-machine," Mrs Garland soothed him hurriedly. It was of such tremendous importance to get that room let. "It's jest a typewriter she 'as...."

"Of course. I ought to have known. Hear enough of them during the day," he added gloomily. "But it's the same thing as far as I'm concerned. I can't work with that noise going on all the evening."

"That's all right, sir. She won't be 'ere long. Got a situation somewhere in the country, living in a gentleman's house."

"The devil she has," thought Stuart; adding aloud, "Is she going soon?"

"Soon enough," Mrs Garland assured him. "Anyway, if she don't go there, she won't be 'ere long. So don't you let that spoil your plans."

The noise of the typewriter overhead ceased; a door opened and feet sounded on the landing. The door of the second floor room was open, and Stuart moved casually to a place where he could watch the stairs. Mrs Garland, fear knocking at her heart, moved with him.

Althea Dennis, coming swiftly down the stairs, caught sight of him and stopped abruptly.

"Why do you watch me?" she asked Mrs Garland wildly.

Mrs Garland frowned. She wouldn't have had this happen, she thought, just when the room was as good as let, for a mint of money.

"No one's watching you," she answered irritably.

"They are," cried Althea Dennis accusingly, "all day and all night. Why don't they leave me alone?"

Mrs Garland, hope almost dead now, attempted to compose her. "You're working too 'ard," she said, "that's what's the matter with you. You ought to sleep more instead of typing on that old machine."

Althea Dennis lifted her ravaged face. It was haggard and wasted; her eyes were wild and passionate. It was the face of a woman undergoing terrible mental conflict.

"Sleep!" she cried. "Why do you talk to me of sleep, I that shall never sleep again? All day he follows me, follows me through the streets, follows me up the stairs, sits in my room and watches me. And at night he haunts me, till I know I shall find no rest until I am where he is now."

She turned and rushed down the stairs as though that spirit of Simon Chandos was behind her, driving her out into the wet miry town. Stuart stared after her. Crazy she might be, abnormal she undoubtedly was, but there had been in that moment, as on the occasion of Chandos' death at Freyne, a certain wild majesty not to be denied. Stuart was reminded of Lady Macbeth.

"Don't you take no notice of 'er," Mrs Garland was urging. "She's a bit odd, she is. Got 'erself mixed up in a nasty case in the papers, and she's bin in the courts, and it's got on 'er mind. Next thing she'll be saying she done it herself."

"Has she ever said that?" Stuart asked.

Mrs Garland was suddenly recalled to discretion. "'Course not. Pore thing! She's all wore out, with worry, that's what it is. I know. I bin bad myself sometimes. Now, sir, about the room. When would you want to come in?"

He arranged to come in the next day, and left the house wishing he could find some excuse for looking at Miss Dennis' room. He went back to the little coffee-house opposite and ordered tea. He lingered a long time over that. But Miss Dennis had not returned when he reluctantly rose and paid his bill. Outside he found a policeman, and him he engaged in conversation, asking for the whereabouts of a fictitious square. The policeman obligingly produced a small pocket-directory of the streets and squares of London, and together they examined it. They had just come to the reluctant conclusion that Stuart must be mistaken in the name of the place when Althea Dennis came into sight. Anxious not to arouse her suspicions Stuart thanked the constable, and vanished round the corner. Taking a passing taxi he drove back to his own rooms; here he changed and then ringing up Mrs Garland's house asked for Miss Dennis. He wanted to be sure that she was still there. After a moment he heard her voice.

"Miss Dennis speaking. Who is that?"

"Parkinson. Good-afternoon, Miss Dennis. You were kind enough to give me your telephone number, so I thought I'd ring you up rather than write to you. I'm sorry to say that I've made other arrangements about a secretary. It occurred to me that you might have some other plan in hand, so I let you know my decision as soon as possible."

Even over the telephone he could make out a note of disappointed chagrin in her voice.

"But—what was it . . .?"

"As a matter of fact, I have engaged a lady who is also a very keen gardener. And at my house at Dovercourt there is a large garden; it will help me—and my wife—very much to have some one with us who understands that sort of thing."

"I see," said Althea Dennis slowly, "then it's no use. . . . Of course it isn't. Thank you for telephoning. Goodbye."

Stuart had a momentary loathing for his profession as he hung up the receiver; but an instant later this was overlaid by his natural love of the chase. Pulling on a slouch hat that almost hid his face he went back to Buryham Square, and lounged slowly the length of the street, covertly watching No. 29, in case the strange man should appear a day early, or Miss Dennis go out, in which case he meant to shadow her, on the chance that she was meeting him elsewhere. But though he lingered in the neighbourhood until eleven o'clock he saw no sign of her. At eleven the lights in No. 29 were extinguished, and walking slowly past the steps he heard Mrs Garland drawing the rusty bolts, and putting up a chain that clanked as ominously as Jacob Marley's. A few minutes later he turned into the Underground Station and went home. Twenty minutes after he had gone the bolts were softly drawn, the chain was let down without a sound, the door opened noiselessly, and a dark figure, who had been waiting for the road to empty, slipped out, no more than a black shadow among the multitude of shadows that thronged the street.

CHAPTER 10 THE WOMAN IN BLACK

Meanwhile, there had been developments at my end of the string. On the day before Stuart's visit to the house in Buryham Square, in the guise of a clerk, I was having tea in my rooms when Kent announced that a lady was waiting to see me. Kent and I are old sojourners. He has been with me for twelve years; and I trust him as I trust few men on this earth. But it seemed to me that this was a departure from his normal tact.

"What sort of a lady?" I scowled, "and why didn't you say I was out?"

"I said I was afraid you weren't at home, sir, but she said she saw you come in half an hour ago, and you hadn't come out since then. Watching the door, I suppose."

"I might be in my bath for all she knows," I complained.

"She said she'd wait till you were free, sir."

I tried to think who it could be; surely not Miss Dennis. What could she have to say to me? It might conceivably be Rosemary, whose respect for the conventions is of the slightest, but Kent would have known her. I even had a fleeting thought of the woman in black, but I dismissed that as improbable.

"I'll come out," I decided at last. I had no desire to find myself walled up with a woman of the Dennis calibre. A tall figure was waiting outside, heavily swathed in a thick black veil that hid her features. But the moment she moved I knew her.

"Good Heavens! Catherine!" I exclaimed. "It never occurred to me it might be you. Why this secrecy?"

"May I come in?" she murmured, "and I'll tell you."

I told Kent to bring fresh tea and waited. It was obvious from her manner that something had happened, something pretty drastic.

"What is it?" I asked as soon as the door closed. Catherine's whole attitude spelt little short of actual terror.

"I had to come," she said in a quick nervous voice, "there's something I had to say that mustn't even be breathed in any public place."

"More anonymous letters?" I demanded apprehensively, and she nodded. Then Kent brought in the tea and we talked commonplaces for a moment.

"Did your man find out anything about the letter?" she questioned, when we were alone again.

I told her the story I had learned from Wareing the previous night. As soon as he heard of the anonymous threats Stuart had installed a man called Jessop at the offices of the *Morning Standard* to find out who called for Catherine's reply. About noon the following day a district messenger claimed the letter, and boarded a 'bus going east, Jessop following discreetly in a taxi. At Whitechapel the boy alighted and deposited the letter at a small greengrocer's shop of the type where correspondence may be left for a trifling fee. For the rest of the afternoon Jessop loitered in the neighbourhood, watching the people who entered the place, but no one came for the letter. As it grew darker and the naphtha-lights began to flare, a suspicion struck him, and crossing the road he made elaborate arrangements for letters to be addressed to him there, giving the name of James Fletcher.

"When can I call for them?" he asked.

"Eight till eight," he was told.

"Supposing I'm later than that?"

"You'll find the shop shut. Never let any one call after eight."

Jessop felt tolerably satisfied that the mysterious blackmailer was not likely to outwit him that way. "D'you ever post letters on?" he demanded. "Never bin asked to yet," said the woman doubtfully, beginning to close the shop. "Ain't twelve hours enough for you?"

Jessop was content to leave things as they stood until the next day. At ten minutes to eight the following morning, carefully disguised, he was lingering near the shop-door. But as the hours drew on and nothing happened he decided on a bolder plan of campaign. So, choosing a time when the woman was momentarily off the scene, he tackled the old man left in charge and asked if any further letters had been received for No. 002, *Morning Standard*.

"There ain't bin no more," said the old man confusedly, and then the woman returned, suspicious and resentful. At first she refused to speak, but at length by mingled cajolery and threats he got at the truth. It appeared that she had been approached by a strange woman in black, who wanted to have letters sent there, and then, on the verge of collapse, asked them to help her. She said she was expecting money from a lawyer, a legacy, and she feared that if she had it sent to her own address her brother would lay hands on it and get it away from her for drink. She had promised them five pounds, half of which she paid in advance. Then she pleaded with them till they agreed to let her have the letter after closing-time, to allay the fictitious brother's suspicions, as he would no doubt have her followed during the day. She named a coffee-stall near at hand, where she would meet them. She had put the notes on the counter, and Mrs Pert, "agin my own judgment, sir," agreed to the scheme. That was all they knew.

"There's only been one letter?"

"Yes. What'll I do if there's another in the morning?"

"Keep it till you hear from me or the Yard. Tell her nothing's come."

"And that," I wound up, "is how the matter stands at present. You haven't written again, I suppose?"

"Not yet," she murmured in an exhausted voice.

"Well, if you do, give us notice so that Stuart may take the necessary steps."

She lifted an ashen face to mine. Her tone changed, became extraordinarily urgent. "Alan, you've got to help me to get that letter back."

I was startled by her vehemence. "I'll do everything I can, of course. I told you that before. It's unfortunate we're so much in the dark. I hoped Stuart would be able to discover exactly who it was."

"He needn't bother," she said in the same tone, "I've found that out."

"That ought to help us. Who is it?"

"A one-time maid of mine called Manvers. I dismissed her for theft, and afterwards—I couldn't foresee this—I didn't feel able to give her a reference she wanted. After all, she'd stolen from me, and it wouldn't have been fair to her new mistress."

"And now she's taking her revenge?"

"Yes. She must, by some terrible ill-fortune, be connected with one of Rupert's ex-service men; otherwise how could she have come across it? For all I know, Rupert's had trouble with one of his people, and they're killing two birds with one stone."

"Does she refuse to part with the letter?"

"Oh, no. Why should she? It's no use to her except as marketable property."

"I suppose she wants a high price?"

"A thousand guineas."

I had been prepared for something pretty outrageous, but that left me gasping. I repeated foolishly, "A thousand guineas? But that's ridiculous."

"Not for me," said Catherine sombrely.

"But the woman must be mad. She must know she won't get that?"

"She will, and knows she will."

"But Catherine—no letter on earth can be worth that money."

"Perhaps not; but Rupert's life is worth even more."

"And you think this could turn the scale?"

Catherine lifted a cup automatically to her lips; she was trembling so much that the liquid spilt and stained her dress.

"It matters as much as that?" I asked again, trying to realise the position. What on earth could Catherine have said that could make the letter worth a thousand guineas, or suggest so preposterous a sum to the woman who held it? It must have been maddeningly indiscreet.

She raised her ghastly face to mine. In those few minutes she had aged, become leaden, dead, dreadful to see. Only her eyes lived, and these stared hollowly, despairingly, into mine.

"I wrote it the day I came back from Devonshire. Oh, we were wonderfully careful, but whenever I went to Daisycombe it was to see him. I had had a week—if Dives had been allowed to come out of torment and lie in Abraham's bosom for seven days he might have felt as I did then. I was beyond discretion, even decency—and I poured out my whole heart to him. Yes, you'd shrink from me if you knew what was in that letter. I said I wanted to be with him always, that I hungered for freedom; told him I could not live without him, and would agree to any plan that would set us at liberty. I said all my future rested with him.... Oh, it was insane."

I was thinking. "You're right," I acknowledged. "If there's really all that in it, it would be fatal. Any common-sense jury would regard it as incitement to murder. It might hang Dacre, and it would condemn you."

"Oh, I'm condemned already," she cried unconcernedly. "I don't count. But if Rupert dies I don't want to go on living. I wonder if you understand in the least or if you just loathe me."

I let that go. "Tell me, Catherine," I asked, acting on an impulse that I instantly regretted, "do you, in your heart of hearts, think he may be guilty?"

"I—don't—know...."

"There's a chance then...?"

She interrupted me. "Alan, I'll tell you something I haven't told a soul. I've sworn all through, and I shall till the end of the chapter, that Rupert was with me at the time the morphine was administered."

"And he wasn't?"

"No." In spite of the fact that this made the case against Dacre blacker than ever I felt blissfully glad that he hadn't fallen so far below his own standards of honour as to betray his friend when he was staying in the house.

"He didn't come till almost three o'clock," Catherine went on, "that gave him plenty of time."

"Then you do believe . . . ?"

"No, no," she cried passionately. "I don't. But he said one thing I couldn't understand. He said, 'It's almost over, all our waiting and pain.' Afterwards, when we discovered Simon, I remembered that."

"And pieced together a story to save him?"

She asked simply, "What else could I do? I love him."

My disappointment after that moment of elation was intense. My sympathy for Dacre was steadily waning; I began to see that Catherine didn't really need it, and in my mind a little doubt grew as to what Catherine had really said in that letter that would account for her terror at the thought of its falling into official hands.

"About that letter?" I resumed. "Are you really considering paying that exorbitant sum?"

"What else can I do? If I write and tell her she's liable to arrest for blackmail she'll say, 'Call in the police.' She knows I daren't. Oh, don't make any mistake about it. She's got all the aces in her sleeve. It'll be bad enough even if I do get it back. She'll have read it, and she can tell the whole world what was in it."

"She won't be able to prove it."

Catherine moved impatiently. "Oh, proof! proof! Proof isn't anything. They can't prove Rupert murdered Simon, but they've arrested him for it."

I abandoned that line. "How are you sending the money?" I queried. "Through the post?"

"She stipulates that it's to be in notes of not more than ten pounds, that she herself will take it from me in a place she will name, and that in return I shall have the letter."

"And you're going to agree?"

"I must. But you've got to help me—to find the money. I've sent for my pass-book. I've got about three hundred pounds, and that's what I'm living on till the executors decide to divide the estate, and they tell me they won't do that till this affair is settled."

I felt profoundly uncomfortable. I wasn't in a position to lend her the money; but she saved my face by producing some jewellery she wanted me to sell on her behalf.

"Most of it," she explained, "is family stuff I can't sell. It would create a scandal. Every one knows the Chandos pearls, the Chandos diamonds. But these are one or two personal things." She opened a small case and showed me an emerald pendant and a necklace of sapphires. "And there's this," she added, slipping a ruby ring from her finger. I remembered Chandos buying that.

"Would you sell it?" I asked tentatively.

"I must." Her attitude amazed me. It didn't apparently strike her as unsportsmanlike to take the jewels Chandos had given her to save the man who might have murdered him.

"Have you anything he didn't give you?"

"Nothing that would fetch anything like the money. I rely on you, Alan. I shall never want to wear any of these again. If I don't get that letter back, sooner than let it fall into the hands of Scotland Yard, I'll kill myself. I won't live to see it sold to the highest journalistic bidder."

At that instant the front-door bell pealed. Catherine leapt to her feet.

"Some one to see you," she exclaimed, panic-stricken.

"It's all right," I assured her, "don't lose your head." But that was just what she proceeded to do. It became obvious that Kent had let in the new-comer. I couldn't imagine who it was, and why he hadn't said I was engaged. The door handle began to turn, and Catherine, absolutely demoralised now, turned with it.

"Where does that other door lead?" she panted, and, like a frightened rabbit, she scurried through the communicating door as Kent came in.

CHAPTER 11 THE WOMAN IN BLACK

I

"What the devil!" I commenced furiously. "What's the matter with you, today, man?"

"I'm sorry, sir, but I couldn't help it," the luckless Kent began, when a voice cut in from the hall, "It's no use cursing *him*, Alan. Curse me, if you must. I said I'd come in. But I'll wait if you're engaged, till you're free."

I couldn't mistake Rosemary's voice anywhere. All the same, I thought it scurvy of fate to plant the two women on me simultaneously. There were so many men in London whose knowledge of women would have enabled them to deal with the situation with perfect aplomb. For myself I infinitely preferred even the sulky camels with whom I had once traversed a particularly unwholesome desert.

Rosemary appeared on the threshold. "Why, there isn't any one here at all. You were just slacking."

I was in two minds as to whether it would be wise to mention Catherine: I didn't want a flavour of scandal to start. But then it occurred to me that she could hear everything we were saying, and if she wanted to come out, she could. In fact, I hoped she would. I was beginning to find the position a bit warm. Then I turned towards Rosemary, and saw immediately that something was very wrong indeed. She was very flushed and her eyes had that hard, direct look they take on when she is angry.

Characteristically she came immediately to the point. "I came to you, Alan, because you're one of the few people I know who will tell me the truth. It's about Scott."

"Egerton?"

"Of course. How many Scotts do you suppose I know?"

"I know nothing about him," I said finally.

"Or nothing you'll tell me?" she challenged me.

"What on earth do you want to know about him?" I asked. "I thought you were in love with him. If you can't trust him. . . ."

"Oh, Alan, stop that mid-Victorian mush," she cried impatiently. "How can I know anything about him? Girls don't, not when they're wrapped in swaddling clothes from cradle to grave, as I am."

I laughed there, which was a mistake. Rosemary was in deeper waters than I guessed. I saw that the next minute and apologised.

"If you've been listening to old wives' tales," I warned her, but she cut in quickly, "Ah, then you admit there are some to hear?"

I had a feeling of being worsted. "I know absolutely nothing about the fellow except that a brilliant future is predicted for him. That type always has its detractors."

Rosemary was watching me narrowly. "I'm staying with Ursula Brent at her boarding-house; at least, they call it a private hotel. When is a boarding-house not a boarding-house? When it's in South Kensington. The sort of people who live in that kind of place aren't rich enough to be ostentatiously vicious, and aren't poor enough to have to earn a living, so they talk. They haven't anything else to do. They go to mannequin shows, and talk; then they lunch together and talk; then they have tea in the lounge and talk; they talk at dinner, they talk in the drawing-room after dinner, they play bridge and talk all through that. They're the sworn members of the worst thieves' club in the world—thieving reputations. Of course, since I left Freyne I've seen a good deal of Scott." She looked at me a little defiantly. "If it hadn't been for Simon's death we should have announced the engagement last week."

I nodded sympathetically, though my sympathy at the moment was for Bannister.

"Of course, Scott wouldn't agree to that, with things as they are. He thinks it wouldn't be *comme il faut*. I said Simon wouldn't care, but it seems that if you're going to be Prime Minister one day you begin practising diplomacy in your cradle. So he said we must wait a bit, and I didn't care. It isn't what other people know about you that matters. But I've met him pretty often, theatres and galleries and so forth. Well, last night a woman in this hotel place—a sort of Persian cat in Parisian clothes—you know the type, Alan, who wouldn't *do* anything immoral for the world, but whose mind is a sink of beastliness. She censors people who do the things she gloats over mentally, in books and theatres and that kind of thing. Well, last night she came over and sat by me. I hate her talking to me. I always feel as if I'd been bathing in slime, because even if I'm rude to her, and I usually am, she doesn't stop telling me stories of all the people in the room—and they're probably all lies."

"What did she say about Egerton?" I asked, despairing of ever getting to the point if I let Rosemary take her own road.

"She said, 'If you will allow a woman old enough to be your mother (only, of course, she's never been any one's mother, though she's had two or three husbands; that sort never is) to give you a word of advice, don't make yourself too conspicuous with young Mr Egerton.'"

"And I suppose you immediately blurted out the news that the engagement was simply postponed, because of Chandos?"

Rosemary regarded me fiercely. "Do you really think I talk to women like that about Scott—or any one I care for?"

I gave up the attempt at understanding her. "But I gather the conversation didn't stop there?"

"Of course it didn't. But I didn't talk to her—she talked to me."

"Is that different?"

Rosemary looked at me oddly. "Alan, what's happened to you? Are you in the middle of an unhappy love-affair, or have you lost all your money? Nothing else would explain your hatefully superior attitude."

"Neither. I'm sorry, Rosemary. But what actually did this harpy tell you?"

Rosemary's face hardened again. "When she warned me against him I said in my coldest voice, 'Really? Why not?' and she said, 'I don't think, my dear, you can know anything about him, or you would scarcely care to be seen about with him so much.'"

"I said I knew nothing to his discredit, and in any case, I couldn't discuss my friends with strangers. I wanted to go then, but she clutched my hand so that I couldn't get away without an actual fight, and cried, 'You poor child, did no one ever tell you of the Daubney case?' What's the matter, Alan?"

For I had started. "So that's where I'd heard the name before," I murmured. "I wondered why it seemed vaguely familiar."

"It must have been pretty notorious for you to have heard of it," observed Rosemary acutely. "Is it true, then, what she told me?"

"I don't know yet what she did tell you," I countered evasively.

"I said I knew nothing of the Daubney case, and didn't want to. So she said, 'I felt sure of it. I knew you were not the type of girl to go about publicly with a man who, having dragged a woman into the Divorce Court, deserted her so that in sheer desperation she killed herself.' I said I didn't believe it, of course, and told her what I thought of her and all her poisonous crowd. Living in hotels and inventing vile slanders. But—is it true?"

"I can't tell you. I was abroad at the time. It happened just after the Armistice."

"What *do* you know of the case? Tell me, Alan. I've a right to know, if Scott's concerned with it."

"I know that Lady Daubney was a very wicked woman, and that, if it is true that she snared Egerton, he wasn't by any means the only one."

"How easily men are satisfied!" cried Rosemary scornfully.

"Personally I think Egerton is to be pitied. She got plenty of men more experienced than he. I don't know just how old he is, now...."

"Twenty-eight."

"Exactly. He was one-and-twenty then, an impressionable age, and she was a most lovely woman."

"I don't blame him for falling in love with her," Rosemary stormed, "he couldn't help that. But to carry on a liaison—she wasn't even separated from her husband. I could have borne that. But they were living together, outwardly anyhow. And he was their guest. It's just what Catherine and Rupert did. That's why I feel I can't meet her again—not yet. If they'd gone away together—honestly. But to take his money, his house, his jewels, and all she got by being the wife of Sir Simon Chandos, and all the time to play the traitor to him! Oh, don't scowl at me like that, Alan. You know it's true. It's horrible. Like Judas Iscariot. And Scott did the same, did he? And then when the case came on, he repudiated it, lied to shield himself, and went abroad. And she—at home—killed herself. Didn't she?"

"I don't suppose for a moment it was on Egerton's account, but she certainly did shoot herself. It was a nine days' wonder."

"And Scott, in Germany, read the papers, and thought how clever of him to get out in time. I don't care how he felt, what it meant to his loathsome career he's so keen on, he ought to have stood by her. I could have admired him for that—perhaps...."

"And you're going to throw him over because of that?"

"Throw him over? I'll never speak to him again. I hate to think I've ever let him make love to me—with a story like that behind him."

"Seven years old," I reminded her.

"That makes it no better," she flashed. "At least, Catherine didn't do that. She and Rupert are sticking together."

I remembered how near Catherine was to us; probably she had heard every word the child had spoken.

"Never mind about Catherine," I said hastily. "That's her affair—and Dacre's. You're not seriously going to chuck Egerton (not that I'm keen to see you marry the fellow) because of that story? It was cruelty to children to drag him into the case at all."

"If he was old enough to be her lover and deceive her husband, he was old enough to face the music," Rosemary flamed. "To me it's the most horrible thing he could have done. I could have forgiven—murder—more easily."

I suppose Catherine, listening to what passed between us, moved restlessly at that word "murder." Anyway, there was a faint crash in the next room, and her voice exclaimed, "Oh, how dreadful!"

I felt more of a fool than ever. To produce Catherine now would enrage Rosemary, who would probably believe that it was a trap to make her betray herself. But Rosemary's thoughts were not self-centred. She paled suddenly, turning so white I had a momentary fear she would faint. But as I moved towards her she involuntarily retreated.

"Don't touch me!" she panted. "Alan, you too! So that's why Kent was so flustered, and didn't want me to come in. How bored you must have been longing for me to go. Now wonder you defended Scott. And Catherine, too. Oh, isn't there one decent man among you?" She turned in a flash and put one hand on the knob of the door, but as she did so the communicating door opened and Catherine called her name.

She, taken at a disadvantage, stared from one to other of us, her pale face flushed, her eyes bright with unhappiness and disdain. I didn't wonder both Egerton and Bannister wanted her. She was vivid with what neither Catherine nor I would ever have again—the promise and colour and fire of youth. I had always thought her pretty; her burning scorn and her tempestuous loyalty made her lovely to look upon.

"You!" she cried, meeting Catherine's glance. "But what are you doing here?"

"My dear," said Catherine mildly, "it might be more fitting for me to ask you that. It's—indiscreet—to say the least, for a girl in your position to call unchaperoned at a bachelor's rooms."

"Because of Scott? It doesn't matter to me now what he thinks."

"Then what I heard was true? You're going to stick to it? I beg your pardon for overhearing, but it was inevitable."

"It doesn't matter," muttered Rosemary, scarlet with confusion and remembering instantly all her candour anent this woman and her lover. "And, of course, if I'd known you were there, I wouldn't have said—what I did...."

Catherine put the incoherent apology aside with a quiet dignity that I found very moving. "I quite understand. You have a right to your own judgment. But, Rosemary, let me beg of you to sleep on your decision. I know more of the Daubney case and Scott Egerton's connection with it than any one."

"How?"

"Because it was Simon who saw him through it. If he hadn't it would have been the end of that boy's career."

"Instead of the end of Lady Daubney's life," finished Rosemary softly.

"Lady Daubney's death," said Catherine deliberately, "was a benefit to society at large. She hated Scott Egerton because he'd escaped her. He was young, and inexperienced, and so provided her with a new thrill. That's why she let Daubney bring the case into court. She meant to have him, mould him, amuse herself with him—and thanks to Simon, he got away. She was rotten to the core—drug-ridden among other things. Would you have him marry a woman like that?"

"He claimed to love her."

"A boy of twenty-one! But, Rosemary, don't forget, if ever I saw a man in love it's Egerton. He isn't the demonstrative sort, but he does care—desperately. It means everything to him."

"Does it?" murmured Rosemary indifferently. Then she added in a cruel tone, "I suppose Alan and you were right when you said that youth and inexperience were attractive. It's no use your pleading for him, Catherine. I've finished with him. I've seen too much lately of the havoc that's wrought..." She seemed aware of the impropriety of her allusions, for she broke off and went out quickly. We heard her ask Kent to get her a taxi, and a minute or two later saw it drive away.

Catherine's eyes, full of compassion, met mine. "Poor child! She's throwing away her whole life for a moment's madness. She loves him and she ought to marry him. What a brute this other woman must be to drag that grisly story out of its dishonoured grave."

"Candidly," I asked, "is it true?"

"I'm afraid it is. Simon thought so; that was why he tried to get the boy out of the country immediately the case was over. He said he was too good to be wasted on a woman like that. As of course he is. She caught him; she was a head-hunter at that kind of sport. You can hardly blame him. All the same, I'm afraid he's done for as far as Rosemary's concerned."

"They're both so infernally proud," I agreed. "Neither of them would eat humble-pie to save a life's happiness. I only hope to Heaven Rosemary won't do something mad on the spur of the moment. What sort of a woman is this Ursula What'sername?"

Catherine shrugged. "I scarcely know her. But she's an intimate of Rosemary's. At this stage I can hardly offer to intervene."

She couldn't, of course; I quite saw that. Besides, when women intervene to help another woman, it is usually a failure. In any case, Catherine had enough trouble of her own.

Once Rosemary was out of sight she forgot her. "You'll help me?" she said quickly. "Sell them for the best price you can get and post me the money—or bring it round."

I promised dubiously. I was beginning to see that a man who is anxious for a measure of safety must choose between marriage (when Catherine couldn't have come down on me), and the wilds, where she couldn't have reached me. Of the two, I felt that my vocation was the wilds.

After Catherine had gone I stood by the table, letting the sapphires run through my fingers. That necklace had been another love-gift of Chandos to his wife, on the first anniversary of their marriage. He had shown it to me the night before, asking anxiously if I thought she would like it. The picture of him, as he had been then, rose up before me so powerfully, so vividly that I tossed the jewels into a drawer and cursed Catherine and Dacre and all those others who had combined to break up a life so noble and so fine.

II

The next day I went to see Wareing and told him of the second letter.

"D'you know the woman's address?" he rapped out. I had to confess I didn't.

"If you can discover it, it would be useful," he said. "I'm almost sorry, though, about this last development. It makes me wonder what actually is in that letter, to make Lady Chandos so broken by fear. I don't know whether you could learn?" He looked at me inquiringly.

"I can hardly ask for permission to read a document of that nature," I suggested dryly, "particularly after Lady Chandos' confidences."

"There's one thing," Wareing went on slowly, "she means to keep it out of court. I hope for the sake of the man I'm defending that she's successful."

When I left him I went to Christie's to have the jewels valued. I was offered six hundred down, and I closed with the offer. I calculated that Catherine must have quite another thousand pounds' worth of jewellery, bar the Chandos pearls, and these she might be able to dispose of on her own account. Then I took the money round to Catherine's flat. She had said that she would be in all the afternoon, so I hoped by calling in the morning to avoid another conversation. Matters fell out as I had trusted, so I left the packet with Peters, whom I knew to be trustworthy, and went round to my club, feeling a fervent need for male society. There were one or two fellows there whom I knew, and we chatted for a short time, making an arrangement for dinner the following night to renew my acquaintance with a chap called Sullivan whom I'd met shortly before the Armistice. Then I glanced at the papers and wished to Heaven I had never come back to England. (I spent quite a lot of my time just then in that vain desire.) As some of the prosy members began to drift in I unostentatiously departed. Anxious to avoid the more crowded streets I turned towards Greyfriars, and in Lincoln's Inn Fields ran unexpectedly against Egerton. He greeted me shortly.

"Afternoon. Have you seen anything of Rosemary lately?"

His cavalier manner annoyed me, and my voice was as brusque as his as I answered. "I saw her the other day. She's still in town."

"Quite. I was aware of that. Did she ask you anything about me?"

"Why not put that question to her yourself?" I suggested blandly.

"I would, if she'd consent to speak to me," Egerton answered in imperturbable tones. "But I met her this morning and was publicly cut. It wasn't encouraging."

"Probably you can furnish a reason," I remarked coldly.

"I don't doubt it. What did you tell her?"

"That my knowledge of you was nil. . . ." I stopped, realising how neatly I had fallen into his trap.

"So she did come to ask you that," he was murmuring, "I guessed as much. But if you knew nothing you couldn't confirm the rumour."

"I didn't," I replied shortly, making signs of moving on.

"Then who did?"

"How should I know?"

Egerton looked thoughtfully at the pavement, and then at his perfectly-cut, flawlessly-polished boots. "Who was it?" he said again. "Lady Chandos? Ah, I thought so. She knew all about it."

He stretched out his hand and took a paper from a passing newsboy and glanced at it nonchalantly, as it lay folded between his fingers. Then he laughed softly, and passed it to me.

"You mustn't miss that," he observed. "Cream of the pudding. The true Romance."

He indicated a certain paragraph in the middle of the front sheet. It was headed "ROMANCE FROM TRAGEDY," and read:—

"The engagement is announced of Mr Guy Allerton Bannister

and Miss Rosemary St Claire. Mr Bannister is well known as a war correspondent and writer on scientific and political subjects. Miss St Claire is the ward of the late Sir Simon Chandos, for whose murder Captain Rupert Dacre is now under arrest. Miss St Claire and Mr Bannister were fellow-guests at Sir Simon's house at the time of his tragic and mysterious death. It is understood that the marriage will take place shortly."

"Got it?" drawled Egerton at my side. "You might let me have my paper back. I want to see the cricket scores. Thanks."

It was an uncomfortable position and I was glad when opportunity offered for separating.

"How these papers gloat!" Egerton went on in the same voice. "Romance out of tragedy, indeed. But I assure you, Ravenswood, that though I may not be able to compel Rosemary to marry me, he shall die before she marries Bannister."

Egerton had presumably got in for the last year or so of the war, and had the average young man's light way of talking of death.

"That's ridiculous," I said curtly. "Rosemary has a perfect right to choose whom she will marry."

"Not as long as I'm above earth," he returned, waving his stick at a taxi, "and if I'm underground you may be perfectly certain I shall take Bannister with me. Goodbye. I have to get back to the House."

It was a baking day in the first week of August; the sun made the pavements almost red-hot; yet Egerton, sitting at ease in a faultlessly-cut suit of pale fawn, reading the cricket-scores as he was rapidly driven through the press of the London traffic, looked as cool and untouched as though it were January. He was, indeed, the one calm, unhurried creature whom I saw that afternoon; no one watching him would have dreamed of the tumult surging in his brain.

*

It must have been about two hours later that Althea Dennis

made Stuart think of Lady Macbeth.

CHAPTER 12 NEMESIS

I

Illogically enough, for I was prejudiced against the fellow, young Egerton's face haunted me all night. I had, indeed, conceived the madcap notion of going to see Rosemary when something happened that made me forget them both.

Kent had just brought me the papers, *The Times*, to which I normally subscribe, and the *Morning Star*, one of those vulgar penny dailies that give first place to scandals of all kinds. But the dignified *Times* had no chance that morning: for the *Morning Star* had a headline right across the page.

STARTLING DEVELOPMENT IN CHANDOS CASE.
SUICIDE OF WOMAN WITNESS

There was a whole column on the mysterious affair, but *The Times* told the story better in half that space.

WITNESS'S SUICIDE

"At half-past eleven last night, George King, an unemployed dockyard labourer, when walking along the Embankment, saw a dark figure, presumably a woman, drop from Waterloo Bridge. King, who is sixty-three, and lame from a recent accident, was unable to make any attempt at rescue, but, finding a police constable, informed him of what had occurred. A strong current was flowing, however, and the body had drifted a considerable distance downstream before it could be recovered. Artificial respiration was tried for more than an hour, but without success.

"The body was that of a woman of about thirty-five, dressed in black; a long black cloak covered the figure and would have hampered any attempt she may have made to save herself; she was hatless. In a handbag were found cards inscribed '*Miss Althea Dennis*,' but without any address.

"A purse containing two pound notes and a quantity of small change, a handkerchief and a letter addressed to her at 29 Buryham Square, W.C.1, were also in the handbag. The letter was anonymous, and ran: '*I will call for the money tomorrow.*' It is hoped that the police may be able to trace some clue from this.

"Miss Dennis was recently in the public eye in connection with the mysterious death of Sir Simon Chandos, for whose murder Captain Rupert Dacre is now awaiting trial. It was Miss Dennis' evidence that was the conclusive feature of the case against him."

The Morning Star, of course, was full of veiled hints about a confession; for it accepted the thesis that the suicide was a tacit acknowledgment of guilt. Scotland Yard, however, had nothing to add; no paper or letter of any kind had been received by them. The body at present lay at the mortuary, awaiting the inquest. Miss Dennis' landlady and Catherine were called for identification purposes. This much I learned from Catherine herself; she telephoned me at lunch-time, asking if I would come down to the Coroner's Court with her. The inquest took place at four-o'clock. It was a very short affair, though a good many curiosity-mongers turned up. Their opinion was unanimous that she had drowned herself, partly because of remorse, and partly because (as the mysterious letter suggested) she was being blackmailed.

Mrs Garland gave evidence to show that the dead woman was abnormal at the time of her death. I saw Bradlaugh on the other side of the court, taking mental notes. He was particularly keen to get the accurate wording of Miss Dennis' wild fears and cries. Catherine identified her, agreed that she had been Chandos' secretary for five years, and told the court that she had heard nothing of her since the arrest of Captain Dacre. But it was obvious she hoped against hope that some definite evidence would arise that would convict Althea Dennis, and set Dacre at liberty.

They brought in the usual verdict—"Suicide while of Unsound Mind," and the court broke up.

"What will happen to her?" Catherine asked me. "She hasn't any relations, has she? Who buries the bodies of people like that?"

I didn't know, and said so. Presumably the money she had saved—for the evidence had shown that she still had a small balance in the Post Office Savings Bank—would pay for the funeral. Where and when and how the ceremony would take place was no concern of ours.

"And now?" my cousin asked, as we drove back in a closed cab; for, despite the heat of the day, the events of the afternoon had induced in us a desire for seclusion. "Don't you see that now, unless she left a confession, which the police haven't discovered, we *can't* save Rupert. She's escaped us—all of us."

"You don't know that she had anything to do with the murder," I pointed out in constrained tones. I had a sinister feeling that Althea Dennis, dead, was going to be more dangerous than Althea Dennis, living.

"Then you take the popular view that it was Rupert? The proverbial case of the rats and the sinking ship. Well, there'll be one rat on deck when the ship goes down. Besides," her voice changed again, rang high and triumphant, "what about the letter? *'I will call for the money tomorrow.'* What money? She killed herself because she couldn't face whatever tomorrow would bring."

"The police won't disregard that," I assured her. "They don't want to hang an innocent man any more than you do. Dacre won't be condemned till every path and byway has been tested and proved a blind alley. After all, he hasn't got to prove his innocence; the Crown has to prove his guilt. And he gets the benefit of the doubt, if there is one."

The taxi was held up in a traffic block just then, and I went on repeating the same futile arguments. It seemed to me, though I did not tell her so, that it was now extremely unlikely that either Stuart or the police would discover the identity of the bearded stranger who had tormented her, or the part he had played in her life.

The last edition of the papers was just coming warm from the Press. A newsboy dashed out of a side street yelling at the top of his voice. I caught the words, "Chandos' Case."

"The result of the inquest," Catherine said, closing her eyes and leaning back against the cushions. "Will this block never break?"

But I saw through the window something that brought me flashing to my feet—great black letters on a yellow ground—a headline that set innumerable heads bobbing out of taxis, innumerable voices shouting from the tops of buses to the newsvendors in the street below.

CHANDOS' MURDERER REVEALED

That was how it ran. I opened the door and leaped out; I was only just in time. The boy passed me the last copy he had. I took it back to the cab and spread it on Catherine's knee.

Althea Dennis had justified her death, after all, for on the front page, under glaring headlines, with an inset portrait of the dead woman, was the confession that should free Dacre and cleanse Catherine's good name.

II

It was a long document, clearly written by a woman in a highly emotional, even hysterical state. It reminded me obscurely of Edgar Allan Poe.

"Day and night he has followed me since *that* night, and has never let me rest. All day he walks with me, and all night he watches by my bed. If I open my eyes in the darkness, he is there, the eye that never sleeps; if I wake in the dawn he has not stirred. In the street he goes before me, turning to beckon me, beckon me to come to him where he is.

"I know now that there is no more peace for me. He has told H who it was that stabbed him as he worked; H has come round to me twice, and has sent me messages. How can I pay him what is not mine? How can I live beset by this twofold menace? H threatens me; and *he* calls me. So I must go to him.

"It was I who killed Sir Simon Chandos. I had to kill him. He had promised me money—five thousand pounds—when he was dead, and I had to have it. When he told me that he would die in nine months I was glad, because then the money would be mine, and I should be safe. I wrote to H telling him that in nine months he should have his wages. But he would not let me rest. One month, he said, one month, or he would tell the story to the world. Merciful Heaven! (though never merciful to me) how could I let them know what I have kept hidden for nearly twenty years? I had to kill him, I tell you. And what did I gain? A little silence, and an eternal agony. And now let H tell what he will. But he will not dare. With my death I buy the silence I could not buy in life. Now let him shout the secret to earth and sea and sky. They will not care. As for me, I shall be locked away in the darkness with my pain and guilt, and I shall not hear. . . .

"I could not get it in time after all. By tomorrow it had to be in his hands, and I could not get it. That foolish slip—putting the pen in the wrong hand—broke up my scheming, I had plotted it all so carefully. I bode my time, waited till the house was full of guests, waited till he should be sorely hurt by the woman he loved, waited till that woman's lover should be there also and then I struck. I had written the letters oh! so carefully. I set a note in his blotter; for if murder were suspected, it must not be I that was taken. All I wanted was the five thousand pounds. And all that work was in vain.

"How I schemed! He left the library on that night—it was to be that night—and I blotted the letter and burned the original at my candle and scattered the ashes to the winds. Up in my room

I penned the last letter of all, the letter that should, if need be, brand Lady Chandos and her paramour. Why should I care for them? Already they had taken from him that which he treasured dearer than his life! And I waited. I heard the guests come up, but still I waited. And the house was very still. It knew what I would do, and it waited for me. 'Not yet,' breathed the walls, 'for he is not yet alone.' 'Hush!' said the stairs, as I stole down, 'lest they hear you.'

"They were all on my side—all. They never betrayed me as I crept—oh, softly, softly!—from stair to stair. I tapped on the door, and he opened it. He trusted me and he had been bitterly hurt. But I did not care. I had to have the money, had to, I tell you. And he was almost dead now, spumed by his wife, dying in agony. And I was merciful, yes, very merciful. Just one little prick, and he who had for weeks known no peace lay back quietly, so quietly that I envied him. I regretted nothing. Had he not always longed for rest? So I left him. I had set the stage; scattered the papers; put the letter under his hand, set the pen in his fingers. How should I remember then that he was not as other men are?

"And I slept. Yes, that night I slept, because fear had left me. In the morning I remembered it all, and still I was not afraid. I watched them beat on the door and call him, and I was glad, because they could not disturb him ever again. I cried out to Lady Chandos that he was dead because she hated him. And when the door was opened it was I who stood closest to him. I who cried my love for him. I that *stooped down and slid the key into his pocket.* Fools! Did none of them recall that of the whole party not one had seen the key standing in the door? It was so easy, so easy that I was almost afraid. They would have left him, but for that man who was not awed even by death. He saw what they forgot—the pen in the right hand—and he knew. I saw his eyes fall on me and he knew it was I. I waited for him to speak, but he said nothing. I thrust myself in his way, I strove to be alone with him that the dreadful thing might be said, but he would not speak. He was too clever. He tortured me as I never tortured the man I killed. He and H—how pitiless they have been to me—he with his secret knowledge whose burden I may never escape, and H who came like a great black evil bird, swooping out of a dark sky to drag me down to hell.

"And then, when they had taken that man away—(for I laid the plot with cunning)—I prepared my story of the dragging step, I hid the seal in my clothes and dropped it on the floor of the dead man's room, I set the finger of justice pointing at him, the man who had stolen another man's wife, had broken the heart that I made sleep for ever—then, then he came back to me. Day and night—day and night—— For it was wrong. I thought I could drug myself. Was he not almost dead even now? But he has come back to tell me that it was too soon, that what I took from him I can never give back. There was work, he cries, that was given him to do, and I stole his time. And tomorrow it will be at an end. H will carry out his threats—does he not always do as he says? There was a night eight years ago. . . . But what does that matter now? All things have come together to defeat me, and I am tired, so tired . . ."

It broke off abruptly there, as though she had been too tired to end it, beyond her scrawled signature.

Catherine was clutching the paper fiercely; her face was dead white, her eyes burning.

"He's saved," she kept repeating, "saved, Alan. And I love him so." I don't think she really knew I was there. She had no thoughts for any one but Dacre.

Peters greeted us with relief. "I was afraid, my lady, you were still down at that court," she said.

Catherine smiled in a vague, glad way. It was extraordinary how her coming changed the room. It looked dead and gray an instant earlier; now it was full of sunlight and spring and colour. Not even Rosemary, eyes afire, cheeks blazing, at the door of my rooms two nights ago, had been so beautiful. No wonder Chandos, poor devil, had lost his heart and his courage and Dacre forgotten his honour.

On the mantelpiece stood a long manilla envelope, addressed in typescript.

"An advertisement, I expect," murmured Catherine, dropping it into a waste-paper basket.

Some impulse made me stoop and rescue it. "Sure?" I questioned doubtfully. "It may be something important."

"You can open it," she said in the same detached way, mechanically straightening the ornaments on the mantelpiece. I slit the envelope, and drew out several sheets of thin foolscap paper, clipped together. The document was typed in double spacing, and seemed strangely familiar. On the top sheet a slip had been pinned.

"I send you this because it is your right.—A.D."

It was a facsimile of Althea Dennis' confession! Ready at the end to make such bitter reparation as she might for the agony into which she had plunged the woman she feared and hated, she made assurance doubly sure by sending one confession to Scotland Yard and a second to Catherine.

"Is it signed?" she asked, looking over my shoulder.

I turned to the back page. Althea Dennis' signature, large and irregular, was unmistakable.

"They must have been posted simultaneously," I said. "Well, in death she has done what she could."

CHAPTER 13 A JOURNALISTIC STUNT

I

That night I was dining with a foursome of men whom I had met here and there over the face of the globe during the past ten years or so, and I did not rise till late the next morning. Indeed, I was still at breakfast when Kent announced young Egerton. He apologised with his usual suavity for the hour of his call. He had, he said, been motoring all night, and had merely stopped at his rooms to change before coming on to me.

I offered him some breakfast, but he refused.

"Take some coffee," I urged him, "it's so infernally inhospitable to feed while your guests prowl about."

He poured himself out a cup, but didn't attempt to drink it.

"I want you to help me," he began abruptly, stopping dead in front of me. "You're the only man I know with whom I can work, and the only one who has the slightest pull with Rosemary."

I stiffened at the mention of her name. I didn't propose to lend Egerton a hand in his love-affairs. "It's in connection with Chandos," he went on, and I stared.

"I thought that was cleared up," I said, tapping the paper at my side.

"I don't care, on principle, who murdered him," the fellow explained. "If a man is killed by lightning, do you trouble which individual flash did it? Chandos is dead. His murderer is so insignificant that he's blotted out by that tragedy. But I do happen to care for Rosemary. She's bent on ruining her life...."

"By marrying Bannister instead of you?" I asked brutally.

"She'll probably mess it up if she doesn't marry me," he answered coolly. "But she certainly isn't going to marry him. By the way, I suppose the morning paper adds nothing new? I haven't seen one yet."

I passed him *The Times*. "You've read the confession?"

"Skimmed it." He read it leisurely, while I tackled the marmalade.

"I fancy that about settles it," I said.

"It's a very pretty journalistic stunt," he agreed.

"What do you mean?"

"Why was it so late?"

I felt nettled. "Thomas wouldn't have stood a chance with you," I returned irritably. "She left the letter with her landlady, of course."

"Has any one said so?" He picked up *The Morning Star*. "I don't see anything about that here. However, we can make sure by asking her. How soon could you conveniently be ready?"

"I don't propose to come with you," I said shortly.

"Not for Rosemary's sake? I'm not asking on my own account. But she's only a child, and a rash one at that."

For the second time I asked him what he meant. His manner changed; he dropped the casual mask for an instant. Under his infernal pride he was suffering acutely, seeing which I capitulated.

"All right, but what exactly do you mean to do?"

Egerton looked at me oddly. "Several things. But first of all, we've got to see the landlady. I rang up a chap I know at the Yard and he says the letter was posted from Bloomsbury *yesterday morning*—some hours after Miss Dennis' death. We'll try your landlady theory first."

There was not, as I had half anticipated, a crowd of unwholesome sensation-mongers outside the door of No. 29. Either it was too early for them, or they had all come yesterday. Mrs Garland herself opened the door, and at first glance took us for reporters, a fact that shocked and disgusted Egerton and amused me.

"Yes, sir?" She waited complacent, and pleasurably disturbed.

"I believe," said Egerton, in a low, correct voice, "that this is the house where Miss Dennis lodged?"

"Yes, it is."

"Ah! I am Miss Dennis' brother. . . ." Mrs Garland's attitude underwent sudden change. She cast one suspicious glance at the young man, saw the wide crape band (the same as he had worn for Chandos) on his arm, and said rather tartly, "'Er brother, are you? Pity you didn't come to look for 'er a bit sooner."

"My sister and I have not been on visiting terms for some years. I had no idea, of course, of the position."

"Well," remarked the woman sensibly, "'tain't much use your coming now, is it, when she's got away from every one?"

"I should wish to assure myself that everything possible was done as she would have wished. Indeed, we have travelled, my brother-in-law and I, at considerable inconvenience to ourselves, from the north, as soon as we heard the news. I suppose it was you who posted the letters?"

Mrs Garland stared. "Letters? Wot letters? I never posted no letters."

Egerton, in his turn, appeared profoundly puzzled. "Oh? I imagined she must have left the letter she wrote to me on the last night of her life in her room, addressed ready for posting and you despatched it."

"Not me, and if there 'ad bin any letters, I wouldn't ha' touched them. Why, she was goin' out herself. Why should she leave the letters behind?"

"It was a mistake of mine. Mrs Garland, I'm afraid this business has been very vexatious to you. . . ."

She took her cue on the instant. "Vexatious? I should say so, Mr Dennis. Why, wot with young men calling from the papers, and dragging me away from the washing-up and the scrubbing and all the lodgers keeping me to ask what he said and what she did and 'ow she looked, and the police and all, I can 'ardly call me soul me own."

"I am indeed sorry. Of course, if my sister left any accounts unsettled or any bill of yours is due, I shall naturally take over her debts."

The last shade of Mrs Garland's doubts vanished. No man would claim a suicidal murderess for a relative, and offer to pay her debts, unless he were the genuine article.

"Well, sir, there's one or two little things I could mention. And there's going to be trouble about letting the room straight away, what with my house getting a bad name and all. Thirty years I've been letting rooms 'ere, and never a word agin me till now."

He stemmed the flow of her grievances. "I quite understand, but I assure you that you shall not be the loser. Perhaps I might see my sister's room? There may be small personal belongings of hers—letters and photographs and what-not—that she would scarcely wish left at the mercy of strangers. You will not misunderstand me?"

Mrs Garland was obviously calculating the utmost for which she could cheat him, and she led the way upstairs readily enough.

"Not that there's any photographs nor nothink lying about," she warned him as she opened the door.

It was a large, rather gloomy room with a sloping ceiling; the paper was drab and faded, the furniture horsehair and cheap deal. On a table near the locked window stood a covered typewriter. The rest of the fittings were what one might expect in such a place. A large shabby bed half-hidden by a curtain of apple-green casement; a painted wash-stand with chipped china appointments, a rag carpet that had once been red, a small yellow chest of drawers, a couple of chairs and a big tapestry chair with ears and arms.

"She was here for some time, I think," said Egerton, his eyes moving rapidly round the room as though he would tear the flesh of its meagre trappings from the bones and reveal them in their horrid nakedness.

"Not more'n a week or two, sir. I think she was 'appy enough in 'er own way, if it wasn't for those 'orrible dreams she used to 'ave. Talking and waving 'er arms about and calling 'Simon! Simon!' though there was never any one there. Of course, I wasn't drawn to 'er specially—she ain't that sort." (That seemed to me to sum up the tragedy of her life.) "But we made 'er comfortable enough."

Egerton glanced at the mantelpiece, saw without appearing to see a snapshot of Chandos that Catherine had taken a year or two ago—a particularly happy affair, that Miss Dennis had framed and set in the place of honour; then he moved on to the table.

"I suppose the typewriter's a pretty old one?" he suggested casually, lifting the metal cover.

"Not much more'n scrap iron, sir," she said so quickly that she would have aroused the suspicions of the merest tyro.

Egerton put the cover on the floor and looked more closely at the machine.

"I suppose this was the one she used to write the confession," he hazarded.

Mrs Garland, agog with morbid interest, said mysteriously, "That's right, sir." Then she came nearer. "But 'oo 'ad the other copy?" she asked melodramatically.

Egerton started. "What on earth . . .?" he ejaculated. Then he recovered himself. "What makes you think there was a second copy?"

Mrs Garland took up a red cardboard box and opened it to show us half a dozen black carbons. The top one had been used; all the rest were new. She took out the first carefully and passed it to the dead woman's pseudo-brother. Egerton held it up to the light. It had been used more than once, but since the work had been done in double spacing, whole phrases were legible. "'Hush!' said the stairs as I stole down . . . a great black evil bird swooping out of a dark sky. . . . There was a night eight years ago. . . ." This was the carbon Althea Dennis had used to make her sinister confession.

Egerton, having held it up to the light so that I as well as he could recognise it for what it was, laid it back in the box.

"How did you discover that?" he asked.

"Well, in a manner of speaking, it wasn't me wot found it. It was one of them newspaper men wot 'ave bin coming and coming and 'indering me ever since yesterday morning."

"Yesterday *morning*?" Egerton's voice betrayed a becoming perplexity. "But no one knew anything about the confession then."

"They knew she was dead, though, and I s'pose they put two and two together. Anyways, the first of 'em turned up soon after arpars twelve. I was dishing up the dinner—one of my young gents is laid up with a 'orrid 'acking corf, and I was doing 'im a bit of mince and rice, somethink that goes down easy and lies light, you know—when the bell rings, and a gentleman (she made obvious distinctions between gents and gentlemen) takes orf 'is 'at and says, 'I believe this is where Miss Dennis was staying?' jest like wot you did." She meant that as a compliment. My lips twitched, but Egerton was too young to appreciate humour turned against himself. Mrs Garland went on, "I says short-like, 'It is,' cause there was the mince getting cold on the kitching table, 'and wot of it?' 'I've come from the Evening *'Erald,*' he says. 'They want a special interview wiv you, Mrs Garland,' 'e says. They're convinced there's somethink more be'ind this than jest mere sooicide,' 'e says, 'and if you can tell 'em anythink it'll be to your advantage.' Well, sir, I seed 'e was a gentleman at once, and it did seem funny-like that she should kill 'erself like that, though I can't say as I was surprised, 'er being so odd and all—so when I'd took the mince in to No. 4 back I come and 'e asks me this and that—'Did she ever 'ave any visitors?' So I tells 'im about the man wiv the black beard. . . ." She paused expectantly, but Egerton only said, "Yes, I know about him. Well?"

"Then 'e asks, 'Does she ever seem 'aunted? 'Ad she ever said anythink to me?' and so on. Presently I says, 'im being a reporter an' all, would 'e like to see 'er room, and 'e says, yes, 'e would, so I brings 'im up and 'e says, oh! so pitying-like (Mrs Garland had read similar tales in the Weekly Boudoir Series), 'There's always somethink solemn about a room where any one 'as suffered.'

'Well,' I says, 'I 'ope the pore thing's at peace at last,' and 'e makes a note or two in a little book 'e 'ad, and then went away."

"Didn't stay long?" Egerton drawled.

"Not very long."

"Did you leave him alone at all in here?"

She flared up instantly. "And if I did—me not 'aving no girl to open the doors as it 'appens, girls being that difficult to manage—wot of it? 'E was a gentleman, I tell you. If there's anythink missing from this room it isn't 'im wot's 'ad it. Though 'ow you can tell, not 'aving seed yer sister for years, is more than I can guess. But wotever was in this room when 'e come in is 'ere now."

"I'm certain of it," Egerton agreed imperturbably. "I suppose this is all the paper my sister had?" He touched a half-ream of quarto type-writing paper as he spoke. "Of course, she wouldn't need much, just something for answering advertisements, etc."

"I'm sure I've never seed no more'n that," replied Mrs Garland stiffly, "but you can look if you like." She stood hands on ample hips, while Egerton unhurriedly opened two other drawers and a cupboard and searched them.

"Quite right, Mrs Garland," he said, locking the cupboard again, "I didn't expect to find anything."

"If you're thinkin' of that gentleman," she cried belligerently, "I didn't leave 'im alone more'n a minute...."

"It doesn't matter," he said, lifting his eyebrows superciliously, "it makes no difference to me, I assure you, if he was here two minutes or half an hour. As a matter of fact, when you first mentioned him, I thought it might be some one whom Miss Dennis once knew—a tall, dark man."

"Not 'im; fair as fair, reddish, you might almost say. Talked with a stutter and wore big glasses."

"And carried a case? Of course. All these journalists do."

I was right out of my depths now; so was Mrs Garland.

"Well, as it 'appens, 'e did carry a case. But why not? Probably 'ad to write it all up on 'is knee in the tube."

"Quite likely," Egerton agreed. "It must be an uncomfortable life, Mrs Garland. And I suppose, when the evening papers came out, he was among the first to return to the scent."

"'E was. 'We was right, Mrs Garland,' 'e says, 'my paper was right. We knew there was more be'ind it.'"

"And was it he who discovered the carbon?"

"Yes. 'E was jest goin' round, like these fellers do, makin' up the story, when 'e see the red box; the drawer was arf-open, as it 'appened, and 'e opened it wide, not expecting to find nothink, and there it was!" She paused dramatically. "O' course, in 'er case she wasn't trying to 'ide nothing, but suppose you was to write a letter and think you'd left no traces and then the perlice was to come along and find you left this."

"It opens out new possibilities," Egerton agreed. "I'll just try the machine and see if it's worth keeping." He took a sheet out of the drawer and, slipping it into place began to work swiftly and evenly. I noticed that he used every key, tested the alignment, set down the make and number of the typewriter, and used both parts of the ribbon. Then, folding the paper casually and thrusting it into his pocket he said, "Not a great deal of wear left in it. Still, one might sell it for a pound or two. I suppose you don't know any one who would care to buy it for a low price?"

Mrs Garland was ready on the instant. "There's a man I know, keeps a little shop, 'e does, and 'e was saying to me only last week 'ow 'e wished 'e 'ad one of these machines. But it 'ud 'ave to be cheap."

Egerton nodded. He appeared to be considering the idea. Then he pulled himself together and spoke briskly. "Well, for the moment we'll leave it at that." He laid a five-pound note on the table. "Will you settle my sister's bills with this? And I should like to rent this room for one more week. I haven't really had time to look through her things now."

Mrs Garland said in subdued tones, "Yes, sir," but her hand came creeping out towards the note, like the greedy waves of the sea that come stealing up the sand to recapture the pale shell that was left there at the ebb of the tide.

II

"Well," I asked him, as we came into the street, "did you learn what you wanted to know?"

He didn't answer me for a moment, and then only by another question. "There are some queer things in this case, Ravenswood. Why should a man draw the landlady's attention to a sheet of carbon paper? It doesn't matter to either of them if Miss Dennis left a dozen duplicates."

"Echo answers why," I murmured.

"Because he wants her to know it's there," Egerton returned sharply. "But how did he know?"

"Saw it, I suppose."

"What made him open the box?"

"Curiosity—happy chance——"

Egerton shook his head. "Because he knew the incriminating carbon was there."

"How could he?" I protested. "And why did he come in the morning when there wasn't anything to learn?"

"To put it there, of course. Mrs Garland, though she didn't know it, talked openly with Chandos' murderer twice yesterday, and he came freely in and out of her house."

I gasped. "It's beyond me," I confessed.

"That was why I wanted to know whether he carried a bag —to conceal the red box; whether he was alone in the room for an instant—to put the box into the drawer; whether Miss Dennis had any more paper, because it's unusual to have foolscap carbons and only quarto paper."

"Are you trying to tell me that you know who actually committed the murder?"

"I think so. But I want to get hold of Bannister too. In a manner, we're all in this. His office is in Westminster, isn't it?" He locked himself into a telephone box, but after a minute he rejoined me.

"As I thought," he remarked, "Bannister's out of town. Hasn't been near his office for three days. I usually have an egg-and-milk at this hour if I have not breakfasted," he added pedantically. "Will you join me?"

I acquiesced, though I loathe eggs beaten up in milk. He waited till they were set before us, and then he said deliberately, "It ends, as it begins, with Rosemary. I warned you that it would. You thought it absurd that I should object to her marrying Bannister, didn't you?"

"There's nothing against Bannister except his age," I demurred sharply. "Can you tell me anything else?"

"Two other things. The first—that he is Lady Chandos' lover, and the second—that he is her accomplice in the murder of her husband."

CHAPTER 14 THE MAN WITH THE RED BEARD

I

Egerton leaned back nonchalantly, but despite the negligence of his attitude his eyes were alert enough as he flung down the challenge.

"You can prove it, I suppose," I suggested temperately.

"I shall—presently."

"In the meantime, does it occur to you that you're rather jumping to conclusions?" I didn't propose to play into the fellow's hands by thrusting the words down his throat, because Catherine happened to be my cousin.

Egerton sipped his egg and milk. "Not I. There's been too much of that, though, since this case opened. And, if I may say so, you set the ball rolling."

"Indeed?"

"Yes. At the inquest. I was a little puzzled until then, but your evidence—you will remember that the coroner was painfully exact—gave me the clue I needed. What troubled me was that Chandos, who could speak so bitterly about a man as you told the court he did, an hour or two before his death, could, three days earlier, have written to him in friendship."

"And my evidence told you . . . ?"

"That he hadn't. There was another thing. He said he was sorry for Dacre because he was obviously in love with Lady Chandos and would never get her. Why should he say that? He couldn't have meant that it would be because he himself would never let her go, because he knew he had less than a year to live. So he must have meant that Dacre was doomed to failure because Lady Chandos had no use for him. That was the first point.

"Then he switched off and talked about decency, and told you that he would set his wife free if it weren't for the other fellow. And you—not unnaturally—jumped to the conclusion that he was still referring to Dacre. But he didn't actually say so, and what he did say led right away from such a supposition He talked of the gallery of women he had had; of course Lady Chandos gave colour to the suspicion by settling down at Daisycombe whenever Chandos was away, and that's not ten miles from Dacre Court. So the gossips put two and two together. Then, she having confessed to the intrigue, no one thought it worth while to inquire whether they had actually been seen together in the neighbourhood. There's no one like your rustic for gathering scraps of talk. There's so little change that he becomes either a mystic or a clod or a gossip—generally the last. And the fact that Lady Chandos and Dacre, who's a kind of Squire there, were being seen together would be certain to arouse lively comment. I made it my business to make discreet inquiries; Dacre's character is that of a recluse, as Chandos himself said; they'd prefer him to racket about a bit, seems more natural. Apparently he spends all his time with his dogs, and hasn't even a female servant about the place. That's the way the neurosis is working in him, and of course. Lady Chandos has fostered it for her own ends."

"I think, until you've definitely proved your case, you would be wiser to let that type of thing alone," I told him, conscious of a sudden burst of loyalty to Catherine, that reminded me of the adage concerning blood and water.

Egerton didn't seem perturbed; it occurred to me that he was the type of man who bets on a certainty.

"Now, coming to the night of the murder. Psychologically, of course, Dacre couldn't have done it; he isn't the type. He hasn't got the imaginative brain that could plan the stage, in the first place. As for the letter, it was utterly beyond him. Bannister should have thought of that. On the other hand, it was exactly the type of thing that would appeal to a journalist's artistic sense—particularly a journalist who had been a war correspondent. Get the effect at all costs. And he—very nearly —did. That quotation at the end betrayed him, though. If you ask Dacre who Sidney Carton was, he'll probably suggest a new bookmaker, or perhaps a dog-fancier. He could no more have quoted his dying words than he could have murdered Chandos. But Bannister, who had been discussing literature with him earlier in the evening, knew that that was exactly what Chandos might remember. But in quoting them he made a second fatal psychological slip. Chandos might conceivably have thought of them, but, being a great man as well as a great artist, he wouldn't have struck such a melodramatic note. Only your born *poseur* goes to death with those words on his lips; it's simply because you're steeped in the romance and the tragedy of Dickens that you can believe Carton said them; and even so, read in cold blood, they strike you as grandiose.

"But more than either of those, there was the dog. Nobody thought of the dog. Bradlaugh didn't, because he didn't realise the truth—that Dacre had trained him to follow him everywhere. He literally dared not be alone without him; and if, by any chance, the beast got left behind, he howled till he'd attracted his master's attention. Now, Dacre had told you that; I heard him at dinner, compared him with Captain Hook's crocodile, whose alarum warned you of his coming. You remember Bradlaugh finding me on the first floor—that is, outside Miss Dennis' room? I told him I wanted to be sure the boards were polished. You see the point?"

"The dog's claws, of course," I exclaimed. "What a fool!"

"Exactly. Miss Dennis was questioned on three occasions about the sound she heard, and each time she said 'The house was perfectly still, and the only sound was that dragging step.' On the other hand, when Rosemary gave her evidence, she specially said that she was doubly sure it was Dacre going upstairs because she heard, not only the lame step, but *also the sound of the dog following.*

"Of course, the obvious answer is that he carried the animal, but while we were waiting for the locksmith to open the door Dacre picked it up and it barked the house deaf.

"Then there was Lady Chandos' instantaneous defence of Dacre; she didn't give the fellow a chance of offering any explanation of his own. It wasn't, of course, to prove his alibi so much as to prove hers. Oh, they stage-managed the affair very cleverly, getting Rosemary to ask Bannister down. Chandos couldn't refuse to have the fellow on his premises, unless he gave Rosemary some reason. And Lady Chandos had effectually shut his mouth. They both recognised that. But what Bannister knew, and Lady Chandos did not, was that Chandos was aware of their relationship. That letter Lady Chandos is being compelled to buy isn't the first Manvers has put up for sale to the family. On the other hand, Lady Chandos was to make it clear to the world that Dacre was her objective; there was to be no suggestion of any link between her and Bannister. Whether Bannister intended the matter to go so far as she carried it by her crazy story about Dacre's movements in the night, I don't know. It was arranged that if suspicion should be raised Dacre was to be suspect. But I suppose Lady Chandos thought she'd save him by her melodramatic confession, and the matter would drift into unsolved obscurity. Of course, she didn't know then about the will. That must have been a shocking blow to her."

"And to Bannister," I added grimly.

"Bannister can look after himself," Egerton answered dryly. "Presently I'll show you how. I was watching Dacre when Lady Chandos made her melodramatic disclosure, and he didn't seem ashamed or defiant as you would have expected; his first impulse was one of amazement. It came as a tremendous shock to him. I was sure, then, that it wasn't true. Lady Chandos, of course, relied on the obvious truism that no woman would so brand herself for a whim. And the bluff passed, as she had known it would."

"And then?"

"He's told the rest of the story in Althea Dennis' confession. You've realised by now, of course, that it was a fake? In an hour or two we're going to prove that also. That's where I shall need your help. By the way, the syringe is a point in Dacre's favour. If he'd been planning murder he wouldn't have chosen a weapon that could be traced to him immediately, and probably not to another soul in the house. He'd have been more impersonal."

"You've got to find the second syringe," I suggested.

"That's one of the things that is hidden at present. Still, there's an adage somewhere about the mills of God."

"With you for the miller?"

"I should certainly grind whole-heartedly. The point about the pen was another mystery to me. Both Dacre and Miss Dennis were so intimate that it was almost incredible that they should make such a blunder. But Bannister was a comparative stranger. It's quite possible he didn't even realise Chandos was a left-handed man. At all events, he would hardly be likely to remember it at such a time."

"And the key?"

"He explained too."

"Sorry to spoil your theories, but Bannister never even came into the room until after the finding of the key."

"Of course not. He was playing for his life. But Lady Chandos did. She leaned over his shoulder, went through all that revolting spectacle of grief; it wasn't hard, when she had her arms actually about him, to drop the key into his pocket unobserved. Bannister was standing by her side all the time the locksmith wrestled with the door. Oh, they arranged it neatly enough. But Lady Chandos gave it away. She so obviously acted her part from start to finish. No woman of her experience gives vent to her own feelings like that in public. Instinct makes her hold on to dignity. But she was a bad actress. She wanted to make us all believe that Dacre was her whole world. All she actually did was to sow suspicion in the minds of most of us. That night in the drawing-room, for instance. After six years of marriage she couldn't have been so far from self-control that she should make such a scene. Chandos must have touched her accidentally many times, and she hadn't shrunk like that before. Otherwise he wouldn't have been so sick and shaken then."

"And Bannister's engagement? Is that part of the plot too?"

"His plot, but not hers. He hadn't any thought of it when he planned the murder. The news about the will came as a surprise. He made up his mind fast enough. Of course, Lady Chandos can say nothing. He's aware of that."

"But even if she remarries, Lady Chandos keeps ten thousand, and that's all Rosemary's got."

"You don't realise. Bannister believes the confession will be accepted as valid. Then Dacre will be set at liberty and Lady Chandos will simply have to marry the man. The fifty thousand she forfeits on marriage goes to Rosemary. What Bannister sees, damn him, is a certain income of three thousand, and a girl who will undoubtedly amuse him for a time. I don't doubt he'll persuade her to make some agreement, which she won't understand but which will give him power over her fortune."

I came back to Althea Dennis; I was groping hazily through this mist of incredible certainties that shook all my faith in my world and its ways. Catherine and Bannister! And he was proposing to marry a girl like Rosemary!

"So that the confession Miss Dennis left behind . . ."

"She didn't."

"And the police. . . ."

"Who posted it to the police? Not she, not her landlady. Then who? It wasn't received at the Yard till she'd been dead sixteen hours. Oh, it was a clever scheme and it almost succeeded. The whole thing was amazingly well-planned. It was Bannister's ill-luck that he was out of town when Miss Dennis committed suicide. The letter had to be posted in London, and when he saw the news early yesterday morning he came down hell-for-leather. But he was too late. By the time he had prepared the confession—and that was extraordinarily good, because it fitted in perfectly with Mrs Garland's evidence—(the journalistic touch again) by that time it was midday. Of course, it was quite likely that the question of time wouldn't be raised. But it was a tremendous risk! All he saw was that the case against Dacre wasn't turning out so well as he had expected. Then came Wareing's suggestion that probably Miss Dennis was concerned in the affair, and he realised instantly that if it could be shown that she was being blackmailed there was an excellent motive for suicide. Remember, the suspicion had already been set on foot. And it's instructive to note that there were no mysterious elements in the case as far as she was concerned until after the first consultation between you and Bannister and Charteris Wareing."

"And the bearded stranger who persecuted her....?"

"Was Bannister himself. He knew that sooner or later (probably sooner) Stuart would call to verify his suspicions, and Mrs Garland would tell him the story of the man who was badgering her for money and driving her half-crazy. It was vital that there should be some such stranger in the case—so he filled the part. Of course, he could hardly have hoped for such good fortune as her suicide."

"And no one was threatening her life or peace of mind?"

"Not for an instant."

"And H, the man who knew the secret she'd guarded for twenty years?"

Egerton smiled faintly. "Part of the journalistic stunt."

"Then how do you account for her cries and delirium, and her complaints of being haunted?"

"She was haunted, terribly, irrevocably haunted. Day and night Chandos lived in her consciousness. She couldn't escape him. She spoke truth when she told us that from the hour of his death she, too, began to die. She'd built all her life round him, and it had no existence apart from him. Her life had been repressed so that she poured every atom of her emotion into one channel, with the inevitable result that it overflowed its banks. She was a mono-maniac; women so often are, because they're denied, by position or education or simply the limitations of their sex, the wider sphere of interests that is open to us. They cling to one idea that they can embrace, and overload it."

"Does it interest you to know that Bannister agrees with you?"

"He knew from experience. Lady Chandos had reached the pitch where the whole of her moral and mental horizon was dominated by him. The murder of her husband, the attempted murder of Dacre, all these were dwarfed to insignificance by her wild and evil passion for Bannister. Where did we start? With Miss Dennis' suicide? Well, she literally didn't find life worth living. Her only hope was death, when there was a thousand to one chance of recognising him somewhere, in some form. Oh, don't make any mistake about her. She was Love Incarnate, that devastating, all-sacrificing unstinted love that women like her pour out like a river to bathe a man's feet. She was wrong and she was weak—no matter what your circumstances you should be master of your life, not its slave—but she was splendid! And as Chandos' wife she would have ruined him; that was the tragedy of it. But his death easily accounts for hers."

"And what do we do now?"

"I've just rung up Bannister's office. They say he hasn't been near the place for three days. Presently we'll go along and verify that. As Bradlaugh says, in these cases we don't presume, we confirm. I have to go and finish off a job for Mountjoy now, but later we'll continue the investigation. So far we've no actual proof, beyond a comparison of the types of two machines—the one Miss Dennis had and the one on which the confession was done. That'll be your job. But not yet."

II

We arranged to meet again outside the House at three. I arrived rather early, and amused myself by watching other people who had also chosen this place for a rendezvous. There were one or two young men, obviously reporters, hanging about, and a marriage queue had collected round St Margaret's. The sight of that recalled Rosemary to my mind. It was horrible to think that she was at Bannister's mercy now. I wondered how Egerton could stand that knowledge, particularly how he could go, with such apparent unconcern, to prepare the memorandum for Mountjoy. The bride came out, a sallow chit whose white satin heightened her plainness. People, largely, I suspected, from boredom, began to press round her. There was no sign of Egerton; I began to feel annoyed. He oughtn't to be so much engrossed in politics that he could let Rosemary run an instant's risk that was avoidable. I grew feverish with impatience. In any case, the fellow was ten years my junior, and had no right to keep me hanging about like this. An elderly Scotchman, with a ragged, reddish beard streaked with gray, and enormous gold-rimmed glasses that made him look like an elderly owl, asked me something in broad Glasgow. I was extremely hot and aggrieved and I shrugged the question aside. He said something else about a braw lassie, but just then the clock began to strike, and I discovered to my amazement that it was only three now. I moved quickly out of the crowd, but as the last chime died away I turned to find the Scotchman at my elbow still.

"The hour has struck," he said in Egerton's voice, "are you ready?"

"What Christy Minstrels' show is this?" I demanded dumbfounded.

"I'm not giving any tricks to friend Bannister in this game," he assured me. "He'll probably guess I'm thirsting for his blood, because of Rosemary anyway. Cross here."

He touched my arm and we stood an instant on the kerb, facing Whitehall. Just behind us a man paused and lighted his pipe. The first match went out in a puff of hot wind, and he muttered something and lighted another.

"What are we waiting for?" I asked Egerton, for at that instant the road was clear.

"We've got it now," he said calmly, stepping off the pavement, "I wanted to be quite sure that Bannister wasn't in town,"

"And who told you so?"

"The fellow who lighted his pipe behind us. Two matches mean all's well."

At Bannister's office we were greeted by his secretary, a rather plain young woman with an efficient manner and pince-nez that made her frown.

"Mr Bannister?" Egerton asked.

"I'm afraid he isn't in."

Egerton looked amazed. Throughout this interview and the one that followed he did practically all the talking. It was a magnificent piece of acting.

"Not in?" he repeated. "But ye'll mind I telephoned this morning. Mackenzie's ma name. There's a matter of collapsible barrels (he rolled a dozen r's into the word) anent which I wad like to speak wi' him."

Against that background of broad Scotch the girl's voice betrayed its cockney timbre.

"But, Mr Mackenzie, I told you this morning that he had been out of town for some days and wasn't expected back till tomorrow."

"Tomorrow?" Irritated stupefaction sat on Egerton's face. "Then—did ye no gi'e him ma message?"

"He wasn't here," she repeated patiently. "But we're writing to him tonight, sending him some papers. I could send him any message you like."

"No, no. Is there no one I could see consairning the barrels?"

"There's Mr Daniels. He looks after things when Mr Bannister isn't here."

"Is he in?"

"Yes, he's in. I'll see if he's free."

As she disappeared Egerton turned to me, murmuring under his breath, "Do ye ken aught of steel barrels?"

I was glad that I could claim to be something of an engineer. Egerton nodded. "That's fine. Weel, and is he at liberty?"

"Will you come this way, please?"

Mr Daniels was a young man with a good deal of assurance. "I'm sorry Mr Bannister's away," he began bluffly, "what was it you want to discuss with him?"

"Ah thocht yon girl said he was oot the noo and wad be back after his dinner," Egerton explained, while Daniels smiled in a slightly patronising manner at this ramshackle man who referred thus to luncheon.

"He's interested, I take it, in the Prenderlast collapsible barrel," Egerton went on. "There was a note in your paper last month...."

"Oh—ah—yes. As you're aware, trade has been trying to find for a considerable time a collapsible barrel that won't leak. There was the Whittaker."

"That," I interrupted, "leaked like blazes. There was a fellow in Africa who tried a sample barrel, and when it was filled with oil —why, the thing was practically porous."

Daniels turned to me benignantly. "Exactly. Now, we hope the Prenderlast barrel may prove more satisfactory. The chief difficulty about it at the moment is the cost...."

Angus Mackenzie rose to his feet. I hadn't realised before how tall he was. He towered over the neat, simpering figure of Daniels. Indeed, in his odd garments, his long beard and his uplifted arm, he looked like a Harlequinade Avenging Angel.

"No, sirrr, the chief deefeeculty is not the cost. Has the patent yet been taken out?"

"It has been applied for. Really, sir..."

Egerton swept on. "The Prenderlast barrel is a swindle, sir. It is a deleeberate duplicate of a model I myself invented a year ago, and which I could not afford at that time to put on the market. The plans were shown to two or three men, and one of them has stolen them. Tell Mr Bannister that if he helps to form this company for floating the Prenderlast barrel, as I hear he proposes to do, I will sue them all—and I can prove ma case."

"Indeed?" Daniels was quite unruffled. I suppose they have similar maniacs strolling in and out of such offices several days a week.

Angus Mackenzie's brow darkened. "I'll no say more the noo. But ye tell Mr Bannister what I have said." And at that he plunged into a technical discussion of the barrel, elucidating small points that appeared to present difficulties, skilfully drawing me into the conversation, until he had succeeded beyond doubt in convincing Daniels that, though he might be a freak, he was a freak with definite engineering knowledge.

"Perhaps I had best leave a note for Mr Bannister," he wound up, looking round.

"There's no need," said Daniels, more respectfully. "But I'll tell him what you say. If you'll leave me your address...."

Egerton left it, an address in Regent's Park, and we came out of the office.

"We'll get a taxi," said Egerton, "'buses aren't safe on occasions like these. Even the taxi-driver may be a hired assassin."

"What have you learned?" I asked curiously.

"What I really wanted to know—that Bannister hasn't been near his office since Miss Dennis drowned herself. So the confession wasn't written there. Now we're going to his rooms. He was a journalist among other things, and it's probable that he has a machine there. Anyway, it's worth trying."

"That girl had a typewriter," I ventured.

"Smith-Premier—long threes and sevens—purple ribbon not too new; box of purple carbons on the table. We want black ribbons and black carbons."

"I see. What made you spill that yarn to Daniels?"

"Wanted to convince him we were genuine. That's the sort of thing that frequently happens. You take out a patent on an invention and half a hundred swindlers leap out of the ground and swear they drew up the plans a score of years ago. I've left no impression on Daniels' mind beyond that of a lunatic (at best) and a scoundrel (at worst). As I'm impersonating one of my own countrymen, he probably thinks the last. When he writes to Bannister he'll say 'There was another of those madmen in this afternoon. We've got his address, and I've promised to write.'"

"Suppose he does?" I asked curiously.

"House was pulled down in the spring," returned Egerton without a ghost of a smile. "I wonder why red beards, particularly unsightly ones, should be associated with my countrymen? They are infernally hot. Cheaper than shaving soap, I suppose. We'll stop here, I think, and put possible pursuers off by drinking tea ruined as only the people of this nation know how to ruin it."

We had stopped at the Criterion; Bannister's rooms were in Oxford Street.

"I confess I'm still at sea," I said as we sat down. "Do you suppose Bannister will have left a copy of the thing on his desk?"

"No, he won't have done that. He left the only copy he had in Miss Dennis' drawer."

Bannister's man, a mournful-looking, impeccable creature, opened the door a few inches.

"Mr Bannister isn't at home, sir."

"Not at home? But I have an appointment with him."

"Not for today, sir. He told me he was seeing a gentleman tomorrow." He began slowly to close the door.

Egerton looked up wildly. "But Ah leave for Glasgow the nicht," he broke out. "Are ye sure he's no in? I was speaking with him yesterday."

"On the telephone, sir?"

Egerton saw the trap at once. Of course, if Bannister didn't want any one to know he'd been in town for a few hours, he'd be careful not to telephone.

"Ah met him in the street," Egerton explained, "and he said if Ah cam' round this afternoon. . . ."

"I'm sorry, sir," the man repeated. "He must have meant tomorrow."

Egerton planted himself squarely in the doorway. "But was it yesterday he told ye he was expecting a man tomorrow? If not, it was never me that he meant."

Wright (the man), taken off his guard, said, "Yesterday, sir, when he looked in for a minute."

"Oh aye," Egerton agreed instantly, with a sigh that seemed a prelude to the bagpipes. "'Tis a misunderstanding. But Ah leave for Glasgow the nicht. I must leave a paper for him. Ye'll let me write it here?"

"Yes, sir. Will you come this way?"

He showed us into a large, exquisitely-furnished room. There were good pictures on the walls, a few unopened letters on the writing-table, comfortable chairs standing about, and—what we both instinctively sought—a typewriter standing on a low table near the window, where the light was strongest.

"So he has a machine?" Angus Mackenzie ruminated. "Wull he mind if Ah use that?"

The man looked a little perturbed. "It's an old one, sir, not often used."

"Then he wadna mind ma using it for his own guid surely?" expostulated Egerton. "I'll no hurt it. But the option on the Prenderlast barrel ends tomorrow nicht. And I winna be here then."

I suppose Wright had heard Bannister mention the barrels, and in any case he had no reason to suspect us.

"It isn't a very good machine, sir," he warned Egerton, who only laughed and said that it would be better than his handwriting. Wright opened a folder lying on the table, to display some typing paper.

"I wad like fine to keep a copy for ma ain use," said the persistent Scotsman. "Has Mr Bannister no a car-r-r-bon sheet I could use maybe?"

"Yes, sir. He had a box. I saw them—quite recently." Which, being interpreted, meant yesterday. But when he began to look through the drawers I realised that there wouldn't be any carbons in Bannister's flat today. They were all at 29 Buryham Street.

Wright, a little warm from stooping, said, "I'm sorry, sir, he must have used the last."

"It's no matter," Egerton reassured him. "Ah can keep it a day longer in ma ain heid, where it's been this great while," and with another sigh that with him did duty for a chuckle, he set to work. All the time he flung comments at me in a technical jargon that occasionally left me baffled, though most of the time

I was in my depths. I didn't blame the man for not suspecting us; nevertheless, he never left the room for an instant. Egerton finished an elaborate memorandum, folded it meticulously, sealed it and said anxiously, "Ye'll be sure and gie it him when he comes back? Whaur wull ye put it? Oh aye, with all the other letters." He glanced at the envelopes rapidly, as he laid his own down on the top of the pile. Then he said quickly, "I'll no get ma train but I hurry," and we clattered downstairs, disdaining the lift. He had slipped something into the man's hand as he passed. I didn't see what it was, but I have no doubt that it was exactly in keeping with his assumed character.

In the hall—Bannister lived on the first floor—he stopped.

"I wonder who lives in the rest of the place," he murmured, walking over to where a board on the wall announced the names of the tenants. He stood there for some time regarding them. "Apparently a stockbroker lives just beneath," he observed presently, "and a doctor above. Dr Ferguson." He raised his voice with the last words, and a tall, stooping man, fair-haired and clean-shaven, who had just come in, started and came forward, peering short-sightedly out of rimless pince-nez.

"I beg your pardon. You were addressing me?"

Egerton was all apologies. "I didna ken 'twas you," he explained. "I hae come a long way through London to see ma friend Mr Bannister, and they tell me he's oot the noo."

"I'm afraid he is," said Ferguson. "He was called out of town unexpectedly. He was dining with me and a friend who was anxious to meet him, in my rooms last night, but when I got back the day before, I found a note on my table saying he was obliged to go north. I am sorry," he added courteously, "that you should have had such a long journey for nothing."

"'Tis a great disappointment," agreed Egerton impressively. "I dinna come to London often, ye ken, and 'tis a long time since we hae met. I am glad," he matched the doctor's stately grace, "to hae met a friend of his."

"Thank you," murmured Ferguson. (I have seen Spaniards exchanging compliments with unabashed dignity, but Ferguson coloured awkwardly, and looked uncomfortable.) "Yes," he went on hastily to hide his embarrassment, "Bannister's a great friend of mine. I've seen a lot of him lately, as it happens. He's been having his flat overhauled, and the place has been noisome—size and varnish, and what-not—so he's had the run of my rooms, and I've frequently come back to find him there."

"Did he no mention my name to you?" Egerton demanded. "Mackenzie—Angus Mackenzie?"

Once again Ferguson looked troubled. "I'm afraid I don't recall it. . . . One's memory is so clogged with names. . . ." He subsided into incoherent apologies. Egerton nodded in a comprehending manner, and we made our farewells.

"In all these encounters," he observed to me, as we came out into the street, "fate holds the last ace in her sleeve, and I have a notion she's going to play it on our side. That was great good fortune."

"Meeting that man?"

"Meeting that man," he agreed. "That answers something I've been wanting to know for some time."

We went on a short distance in silence. Egerton did not offer explanations, and I did not care to ask for them. Then he said, "It's your show now. This thing has to be proved beyond a doubt. Take this," he pulled a crumpled bit of paper out of his pocket, "this is a spoilt sheet I've just typed on Bannister's machine. And here's the other that I typed on Miss Dennis'. It won't be hard for you to see the copy of the confession Lady Chandos has, and compare notes. You can tell at a glance that these machines are entirely different; and it's all Lombard Street to a china orange that this," he tapped the first of the two papers, "will be your answer."

"You're not taking them direct to Scotland Yard?" I wished myself that he had. It would be so much easier for Catherine, for Rosemary, for me.

But he shook his head. "I don't want Bannister shadowed or arrested—yet. There are other things we have to learn. And I mean to make a clean job of it."

"And Rosemary? You realise every day's delay makes things more dangerous for her?"

He looked at me queerly, as if he were debating whether or no he would break my neck. Then he said, in his usual calm voice, "Yes, I realise that. But there are other things—the anonymous letters, for instance."

"Have you been spending day and night on this job?" I asked curiously.

"I haven't the opportunity," he answered gravely. "Mountjoy has just discovered that he's got V.D.H., which means the end of politics for him. But there are other sleuths in London besides Stuart."

"But if Mountjoy's retiring...."

"There's still the constituency at Cattering to be considered."

"You mean—you're putting up for it?"

"I am. That is, I've been asked."

"You'll accept, I suppose."

Again he shot me that odd look. "I'm marking time for a few days to make sure they really want me."

"Why shouldn't they?" I questioned densely.

He smiled, but didn't reply and suddenly I understood. If he were successful in bringing Bannister to book, he would get more publicity than he wanted; it was conceivable that the Daubney affair would be mentioned *en passant*, and the Conservative Association might prefer to pass on their offer to some one less likely to figure in the sensational press.

I recalled what Rosemary had said. "When he cares, it isn't for a day." She did mean more to him than his career, after all!

Egerton was watching me, smiling that faint, crooked smile. "You see? Still, the Liberals aren't so hidebound as the rest of them."

"You're standing for them?"

"I am."

"But Cattering has returned a Conservative for thirty years."

"High time it had a change."

"A three-cornered fight, I suppose?"

"Unless the Independent fulfils his threat and makes us Puss in a Corner."

"Who loses, if he does?"

"His Party, as a rale—the Election stakes. Coming back to Bannister, there was one thing more. I don't know if you noticed the letters on the table. There was one from Philibert—tells its own story."

"Philibert?"

"Oh, that's not his real name, but it's the one he goes by in every big house in the City. He's the big money-lender, and it's his open boast that once he gets any one into his clutches he never gets away. He's got Bannister—no wonder he wanted money. It's what I've suspected all along the line."

"Hasn't the case gone far enough for you to act?" I asked urgently.

"I've got to have every possible atom of evidence. If the matter were brought against him, and failed, Rosemary would marry him to justify him in the eyes of the world. And then," he concluded regretfully, "I should have to knife the brute—which would be a pity, from my point of view and hers. There are so many better things for us to do."

CHAPTER 15
THE WOMAN IN BLACK AGAIN

I found Catherine in, and alone; also she seemed glad to see me.

"I've got it," she breathed, as soon as the door was shut.

"Got what?"

"The letter. I got it this morning."

"Oh, yes." I'd forgotten it in the excitement of Miss Dennis' death and disclosures. "But did it matter so much now?"

"Of course it did. I wouldn't have had that fall into unfriendly hands for all the money Simon left me."

"Did she bring it to you?" I asked, remembering Wareing's hint.

Catherine shivered. Her face became set, her words slipped reluctantly from her colourless lips, as though she hated to let them escape.

"No. Alan, it was vile. She piped the tune—and I danced. Danced all down to Walham Green, where she has a tiny flat."

I smothered an ejaculation. "Did she have the infernal cheek to drag you down there? A woman who'd once been your servant?"

"Yes. She lives in one of those gaunt, pitiless buildings—Amersham Crescent it's called. She said that if I wanted the letter I must go down and fetch it, and when I arrived she had a girl to open the door, and I was told she wasn't quite ready, and would I wait—in the hall, Alan. Oh, it was horrible, but I'd have faced anything to get that back. So I waited quite a long time, and at last she came out and stood looking at me, with one hand on her hips, her face white and her lips curled back. She smiled at me. She meant to make me suffer all she could. She called me 'My Lady,' with every breath she drew, to emphasise the position between us. Oh, she was insolent, but I didn't dare resent it, not till she'd counted the notes, and I'd got the letter—seen it with my own eyes. Then I kept feeling something would happen—having got my money, she'd get the letter back by some evil means. Every time the taxi slowed down I thought some one would leap on the foot-board, and wrest it from me. But I got home at last, and I burnt it, burnt it to ashes and sifted them to the winds. He's safe at last."

"Yes," I acquiesced mechanically, "safe at last."

Catherine was trembling violently. "But it's only since that letter was burnt that I've realised that she'll always be a vampire to feed on my flesh. I'll never get away from her. I know the type. Even Althea Dennis' confession won't free me."

"By the way," I said, as though the idea had just struck me, "there was one point she didn't clear up in her letter, and that was how she got the morphia."

"Didn't she?" murmured Catherine. "I don't remember."

"That may be why they haven't released Dacre yet," I added.

"I don't understand." She stood looking at me, until a new, horrified look came into her eyes. "Alan, you don't mean they might believe he gave it her? It's wicked even to suggest such a thing. I'm sure she says something about getting it in that paper of hers."

"I don't remember it," I said doubtfully. "Have you got your copy here?"

She fetched it and handed it to me. I read it carefully. There was no question that this could have been typed on Althea Dennis' machine. Even the size of the letters was different. The letter had been typed on thin, stout Denison Bond paper; there were various noticeable characteristics about it. The "E" had slipped a trifle and appeared a shade lower than the other letters; the alignment was faulty, so that the whole had a sketchy appearance; the type was rather blurred, as though the machine had not been cleaned for some time. The capital "C" faded into nothingness half-way down, and in each case it had jumped a little above the level of the other letters. While I was reading the telephone rang, and Catherine went into the tiny closet where it was installed; I pulled out Egerton's memorandum. The paper, in size and make, was identical. There were the same deficiencies, the same slight unevenness of the letters, the same peculiarities that marked the confession. I slipped the memorandum back into my pocket, and listened. Catherine was still speaking. I unfolded the rough sheet we had taken that morning from the bed-sitting-room in Buryham Street. Here the type was much blacker; it was more clear, sharp, rather larger. The stops were very much worn, so that they penetrated the paper; here the capital "C" of which Egerton had typed several, was very clear and distinct. The alignment was more perfect, but the small "D" had worn thin and was only partly visible. I had established what Egerton wanted to know.

When Catherine came back I gave her the letter. "As I thought, she doesn't say anything. Still, I expect it's only a matter of hours now. If I hear anything about Dacre, of course I'll let you know."

That night I took Egerton my news in person. He nodded when he heard.

"I thought as much. Lady Chandos was just as eager to get hold of that letter, even *after* Miss Dennis' confession, you see? In fact, it was more important than ever."

"Scarcely more important," I demurred, "if Miss Dennis' confession could clear Dacre, then even if this harpy produced her letter it couldn't do him any harm."

Egerton looked at me searchingly. "Dacre? What's he got to do with it?"

"Well, it was his letter, wasn't it?"

"Haven't you realised that yet? Of course, it wasn't Dacre's letter. Why should Lady Chandos be mad with terror at the idea of any one reading it? When she heard of Miss Dennis' confession, which she knows is faked, she saw that whatever happened now there would always be two people who would know the truth. One was Bannister, to whom the letter was written, and the other was Charlotte Manvers, in whose possession it was. I don't doubt, in her wildly irresponsible feminine way, she'd made the final arrangements by letter, and that would have given the whole scheme into the hands of the police. And they'll both of them present their bills, Bannister by marrying Rosemary and securing the sixty thousand, and Manvers by bleeding Lady Chandos white for the rest of her days."

I tried to grasp the full devilry of the position. Bannister! Of course, that was why she had spoken so urgently. "If any one should learn that it is Bannister, and not Dacre to whom the letter was written, who was my lover...." That was her thought. No wonder she was half out of her mind.

Another consideration smote me. "But how the deuce did this woman get hold of the letter?" I demanded.

"From the man to whom they were sent."

"Bannister? Oh, that's impossible. He wouldn't dare, for his own sake."

"On the contrary, it was about the safest way he knew of raising the necessary funds. This woman is in his pay, of course. One of the gallery, no doubt. He's desperately hard put to it for money. Here's a weapon lying ready to his hand. Lady Chandos will never guess. And he knew that she'd pay any price he named. It's not as though she could play even her rotten game with a straight bat, as, to do him justice, Bannister very likely will. Though she could connive at murder. Lady Chandos would never face suicide. Now we've got to discover the links that bind Manvers to Bannister. Then our case is pretty well complete. There are probably other letters, too, that he'll stick to in case of the proverbial rainy day. With a little wisdom we may be able to get our hands on those, also."

"And the morphia?"

"Oh, that's easily explained. He copied the trick of a man

who was hanged a good many years ago for murdering various unfortunate women by asking them out to dinner, and putting the stuff in their food. Homicidal mania, of course, but I'm glad to say they strung him up for it. He probably wouldn't have been discovered, but in his foolhardiness, after he'd disposed of about half a dozen women, he wrote to the papers, denouncing the police for their blundering methods, and they justified their reputation by tracing him by the note-paper he used. When they ran him to earth they found he had rooms under a doctor, and had purloined a quantity of hyocene or some such poison. Bannister drew his lesson from that."

"Ferguson!" I cried, light breaking in on me.

"I should say without doubt. He's had the run of the rooms, both when Ferguson was in and when he wasn't. Presently I'll get a man from the Yard to go round there and ask Ferguson to find out if his stock of morphia has been tampered with. But the woman in black is the next problem, and even she must wait till tomorrow."

"Bannister comes back tomorrow," I reminded him.

"I know. We shall have to wait till we're sure he's out of the way.'

But neither of us guessed what the next twenty-four hours would hold.

CHAPTER 16 A RACE AGAINST TIME

I

The next morning Egerton was busy with his chief until midday, when we met by arrangement at Hatchett's for lunch. He was a little late for the appointment. Mountjoy, he explained, had a good deal of correspondence and outstanding work to clear up before he went abroad.

"I'm afraid," he went on regretfully, as we tackled a mixed grill, "we've about reached the end of our tether. That is, we can't, on our own account, get much forrader. We shall have to take Scotland Yard into our confidence, but I think I'll wait till tomorrow. A few hours aren't likely to make much difference. Particularly, I want to get in touch with this mysterious woman, and prove beyond all doubt that she is connected with Bannister."

"Another disguise?" I asked.

"I don't quite know. We shall have to tread very warily. The fellow is presumably back by now, and we don't want to give him a chance of double-crossing us."

We finished lunch and paid our bill, and came up into the cloudy, warm street. By the gates of St James's Church a little knot of people had collected.

"Another wedding?" murmured Egerton. "We'll hope this bride is better-favoured than the last."

Then the couple came out of the church, and for a moment I

was rigid with horror. *For they were Rosemary and Guy Bannister!* The instant passed, and I turned to my companion. For the first time he was taken completely off his guard. His lips were moving, and I caught words that I'd heard in the trenches, but seldom anywhere else. His face was almost black with a dark rush of blood, and the effort he made after self-control.

I made a blind dive across the road, but was restrained by a firm hand on my arm, and dragged almost from under the wheels of a lorry.

"No use qualifying for funeral expenses," said Egerton's smooth voice. His powers of recovery were amazing. The language of the lorry-driver, and the additional advice of the superfluous policeman who always springs up on such occasions, had attracted Rosemary's attention, and she leaned out of the taxi-window, signalling to us in a manner that arrested the notice of every one in the neighbourhood. We came across together. Rosemary's greeting of Egerton was constrained, and she turned to me almost immediately. I fancy Bannister wasn't best pleased at our unexpected appearance, though he masked his feelings successfully enough.

"I've been trying half the morning to get you on the 'phone, Alan," Rosemary said eagerly. "It was all arranged in such a hurry. But Kent said you were out and wouldn't be back to lunch."

"If I'd had any idea of your precipitancy, I'd have stayed in all the morning," I assured her truthfully. "But I thought this wasn't coming off for a few weeks, anyway."

"It wouldn't, of course, in the usual way, But Guy came back last night a day earlier than he'd intended; he's got to go over to Germany for some months for his paper—something metallurgical, that I don't understand. But he couldn't wait, and it seemed a pity to be separated so long, when there wasn't anything to wait for. I wouldn't, you know, have done it if Rupert had still been under suspicion. Would we, Guy?"

She slipped her hand into his, smiling up into his face. That smile troubled me. It was a little nervous, as though the unexpected meeting with Egerton had disturbed her. I saw Bannister's hand close over hers, and felt the sudden trembling of Egerton's tense young body.

But when he spoke his voice was casual enough. "When do you sail?"

"This evening—from Dover."

"Five-thirty boat, I suppose? I wonder you didn't fly over?"

"I did want to, but it makes Guy sick."

Bannister broke in, a trifle acidly, "There'll be no flying tonight," and Egerton responded, "True. Well, if you've got a train to catch, Ravenswood and I mustn't keep you. Good luck, Bannister."

The bridegroom took his defeated rival's hand readily, and there was a hint of admiration in his eyes for the other fellow's good sportsmanship.

"Alan," exclaimed Rosemary in a quick, impulsive voice, "wish me luck."

"The gods watch over you," I murmured, and then Egerton held out his hand to her. She took it nervously, saying in a hurried voice, "Goodbye, Mr Egerton," But he answered tranquilly, "*Au revoir*, Rosemary," She flinched at that familiar name on his lips. But he couldn't call her "Miss St Claire" any longer and he wouldn't use Bannister's name.

He stood watching the car till it was out of sight, then he turned to me. "It's not quite two," he said. "They sail at five-thirty; that gives us three hours and a half. But you have to remember that they'll be in Dover while we're in London, so it isn't really more than three hours. We'd better see Bremner at once. It will be touch and go."

Fortunately, we found Bremner (Egerton's friend at the Yard) in his office. I don't know what pull Egerton had there, but Bremner didn't seem surprised to see him. Egerton explained the position, producing such proof as we had. Bremner still didn't seem surprised; either he was used to the shocks of crime, or he was accustomed to Scott Egerton.

"The time's pretty short," observed the latter, "we've got to get them at Dover."

"There's no extradition law these days," Bremner assured him, "if they do get to Germany we can follow them."

Egerton's expression was inscrutable as he replied, "Tomorrow will be too late. We've got to get them before they sail. That man's a murderer."

Bremner seemed to understand him. He dropped one hand lightly on his shoulder. "All right, Scotty. Don't sweat. We'll get them for you within the time."

But when he heard the whole story he frowned. "Not too much to go on," he remarked.

"The typewriter."

"Yes. But I'd like something more solid than that."

"The morphia."

"That's more to the point. Hallo! There goes the Chief. I know his step. Come along."

To the man to whom such stories as ours were the natural concomitants of life, Egerton repeated his theory.

"This fellow, Ferguson, has rooms just above Bannister, has he? We'd better telephone to him to stay in. Then Bremner can accompany you two gentlemen and the test can be made. Take two men with you, Bremner. Pick your own. Then you can search Bannister's flat for possible communications between him and Lady Chandos and him and Manvers. You'll want a search warrant for his flat and for hers. And a warrant for his arrest, if the evidence is strong enough."

So the five of us piled into a taxi, and drove off towards Ferguson's rooms. We had already discovered that he was in. His voice had been mystified but not anxious.

"It isn't likely he's in it," Bremner said as we swung round the corner and came to a halt.

"There's one possible check that's occurred to me," Egerton put in, "and that is that Bannister has been getting morphia on a doctor's prescription, possibly on Ferguson's."

"And the syringe? That's a part of the mystery we haven't solved yet."

"That bothers me a bit," Egerton acknowledged. "I'll try and piece it together, James, while you're interviewing our medical friend."

I suppose, really, the examination didn't take an unduly long time, but to Egerton and me, waiting in a stuffy little room at the end of the passage, it appeared endless.

Ferguson was clearly taken aback by Bremner's errand. Whatever he had suspected, it hadn't been murder. He agreed instantly to the suggested test of his morphia supply, and there followed a silence, broken at last by a sudden oath ripped out on a note of excitement.

"Short measure?" asked Bremner sharply.

Ferguson nodded, and plunged into technicalities. "More than enough to kill one man," he said.

"Now, think carefully," Bremner went on, "is there any one who has the run of these rooms besides yourself? You have an assistant, perhaps?"

"I have a qualified nurse, who acts as my secretary during the morning. But she went away at the beginning of July, and contracted some sort of fever, so that she isn't back yet."

"You haven't employed a substitute?"

"No. By the time you've trained a new woman, the first one comes back."

"Have you noted your stock since her departure?"

"On the following Saturday. It was too wet for golf."

"That puts her out of court. Is there any one else?"

"The woman who cleans my rooms, but I invariably keep everything locked up, and in any case I doubt if she is intelligent enough to abstract morphia."

"Probably not. Is there no one else? No non-professional acquaintance perhaps?"

"No one," began Ferguson in perplexity—and stopped dead.

Bremner was on to him, like a hawk on to a field-mouse. "Well?"

"There's a man called Bannister—Guy Bannister, the scientific journalist. He's been in and out of the place a good bit this summer. But—no, that's ridiculous. He isn't that type at all."

"Has he ever been here when you were, perhaps, momentarily absent, but when either your keys were available or your stores unlocked?"

Ferguson made a vague gesture. "It's possible—quite possible. I might go to answer a telephone. I shouldn't carry my keys with me, if I happened to have them in my hand. Oh, yes, it could be done easily enough. But surely you don't suspect . . ."

Bremner interrupted him, "One more thing. Has he tried to borrow money off you at all?"

Ferguson was clearly uncomfortable. "I lent him a small cheque recently," he admitted.

"Small?"

"A hundred pounds. He was unexpectedly stranded."

"And it's been repaid?"

"Certainly."

"Ah! I wonder if you could tell me the date."

"As a matter of fact, it was this morning. He came up here early and told me that he was going abroad immediately for his people."

"Cash or cheque?"

"Cheque, of course."

"Have you got it there by any chance?"

Ferguson produced it. It was post-dated two days. Bremner regarded it thoughtfully.

"Not paying it in yet," he suggested at last.

"Day after tomorrow."

"Of course. It's only fair to warn you that you may be subpoenaed at the trial. Thank you, Dr Ferguson."

"It would be interesting," he observed, rejoining us, "to know whether at the moment there's anything in Bannister's account. Manvers only got Lady Chandos' thousand guineas yesterday. Probably he's keeping most of them for his honeymoon expenses. I want to find out the numbers of the notes Lady Chandos gave this woman, and the numbers of the other notes Ferguson's bank gave Bannister. I'll set a man to telephone while we search Bannister's rooms."

"You're sure," I suggested tentatively, as we filed down the stairs, "that he'll have left the letters behind?"

"What else could he do with them?" asked Egerton simply.

"Take them with him. He could lock them up somewhere in his baggage. It's a bit risky leaving them to the mercy of his man or any one who may take a fancy to the place."

"There's bound to be some risk," Egerton acknowledged sombrely. "But it's the lesser evil. Suppose there was some accident. One can't tell. And Rosemary went through his papers. It might be necessary. Obviously, he daren't take even the remotest chance of that happening, Here, it's extremely unlikely that any one will examine his papers at all."

"He might have sent them to his bank."

Egerton considered that. "No," he said at last, "I think not. He'd argue that if, by some extraordinary chance, suspicion should fall on him the first thing the police would do would be to examine everything he'd thought sufficiently important to send to the bank for safety. Whereas, if he kept them in his rooms, it was an even chance they'd be overlooked."

"I'll send a man round to the bank all the same," Bremner put in. "But I fancy your reasoning will see us through, as usual." He nodded at Egerton and went away to give the necessary instructions.

"He might have destroyed them," I hazarded for the third time.

"Not likely. He must keep something to protect himself against Manvers' blackmail. No, I'm not afraid of that, but he's so damned crafty that he'll probably give us the deuce of a search for them. And time presses."

Bannister's man proved hostile. Even after Bremner had produced his warrant he showed a strong disinclination to let us enter. But Bremner wasn't standing on ceremony.

"When Scotland Yard says it's so it is so," he warned him. "If you don't stand aside instantly you'll find yourself arrested, and you'll give the ratepayers a run for their money."

Wright reluctantly stood aside, scanning us all suspiciously as we passed. I was the last of the file, and he recognised me on the instant, and muttered something venomous.

"Might ha' guessed you and that Scot was up to dirty work," he snarled. Fortunately, the others didn't hear him; or, if Egerton did, he didn't think it sufficiently important to take any notice.

I had thought that Bradlaugh's examination of Freyne Abbey had exhausted the powers of investigation. But Bremner showed me my folly. The room looked much the same as it had done the previous day. A few more letters lay on the table, and these Bremner examined keenly. Two or three were obviously private letters from friends or subscribers to the barrel enterprise; there was a large envelope from a press-cutting agency, a bill from his tailor, a couple of advertisements, and a letter in a woman's hand, semi-educated, affected, full of little twirls and twists. Bremner opened it with a penknife with such skill that it would have been difficult to tell that it had been tampered with.

"Not likely to be the one we're after," he observed, "but we're taking no risks this trip."

A single glance at the letter confirmed his view. He looked rather sick and put it back in the envelope.

"Another of the gallery?" Egerton asked, not offering to touch the thing.

Bremner nodded. A pulse in Egerton's temple was throbbing furiously. I wondered how he restrained himself from tearing hell-for-leather down to Dover, and carrying Rosemary away from such vile custody. Even I, who was not in love with her, was shaken and disturbed. The investigation continued. From the waste-paper-basket Bremner picked out an envelope from "Philibert."

"No wonder he needed money," he remarked, sifting the odd papers for a chance of finding fragments of the letters. But Bannister knew his job better than that.

At that moment one of his men returned from the telephone, which was in the hall, with the numbers of both sets of notes. Bremner took them silently; at the moment they helped us no whit.

Meanwhile, the search went on. . . . Every paper in the drawers was examined; the lock of the roll-top desk was picked, the secret drawer discovered, every file carefully scrutinised, and then investigation made for some false bottom to a drawer or hidden panel where the fateful letters might be hid. The clock ticked on. . . . It was already after four, and by five, at latest, we must have found what we sought. Bremner passed into the bedrooms; we could hear him opening drawers and cupboards; he took the bed to pieces, examined the chairs with minute exactitude. They were heavy, old-fashioned affairs, and there had been cases within his experience when they had proved excellent hiding-places for such dangerous documents. But with no result. He came back, a little flushed from his exertions as the telephone bell jangled.

"Right, Pond," he said shortly, to his assistant, who had moved in the direction of the instrument, and then he lifted the receiver.

"That fellow I sent down to the Bank," he explained a moment later. "You were right, Scotty. A dead horse, I'm afraid."

Egerton said nothing. For myself, I felt almost desperate. What he would do if the boat did sail I dared not imagine, murder was the most merciful thought in his mind. He was leaning back in a chair, smoking cigarette after cigarette, staring at the ceiling, that had been hand-painted in a design of fauns and cherubs. The walls of this room were exquisite; hand-painted also with gods and satyrs and figures from ancient folk-lore. I glanced helplessly from one to other of them, thence to the Chinese bronze standing on the piano, and beyond that to the machine we had used the previous day. And I saw no hope anywhere! The clock began to strike. A quarter to five! In a few minutes Rosemary and Bannister would leave the hotel where they'd been having tea and go on board. Bremner hadn't ceased work for an instant. He, too, was troubled, not merely by his own failure but on Egerton's behalf.

Suddenly Egerton leaped to his feet. "It's in here, James. I'm certain of that. If I had the intelligence of a louse, I should know where." He was striding up and down the room now. "There's a story by Poe called *The Purloined Letter*. Our answer is much the same as his." His eyes wandered once more round the room; then he went on, more to himself than us, "In a letter-rack—an old letter turned inside out—and they waylaid him—and searched him—ran gimlets into the chairs—took up his carpet...." He stiffened suddenly.

"May God forgive me!" he cried with unexpected passion. "Of course!"

In an instant he was by the writing-table, had tossed aside the other letters, and had caught up the big envelope from the press-cutting agency.

"The clever devil!" he muttered, "the damned fiend!" He didn't wait for Bremner's knife this time, but ripped the thing open and poured a collection of letters and papers on to the table.

"Why didn't I think of that before? The very place, of course, where only a fool would look for them."

"A fool?" I echoed.

Egerton turned to me solemnly. "The foolishness of God is wiser than the wisdom of men," he quoted oracularly. He was, I think, a little overwrought.

Bremner was already glancing through them rapidly. One fell a little apart from the rest. It was a receipt for £100 from Charlotte Manvers.

"Ten per cent.," he muttered, taking the telephone receiver from its hook. First of all he dictated a telegram. Then he called for the head office of the Dover Police.

"Scotland Yard speaking," he said, "extremely urgent."

"We shan't have to wait long," he added, turning back to us; "anyway, we shall stop them from boarding."

"Sure there's time?" Egerton murmured.

"We shall just do it."

Egerton turned away to the window. One of Bremner's assistants, coming over to him, said respectfully, "You've done this sort of thing before, sir?"

Egerton looked exhausted now. "Secret Service in the war," he returned. And then to me, "That's where Bremner and I met. He liked it enough to take it on afterwards. I didn't. It's a rotten job, hounding men. I'd rather legislate and succour them."

"Those letters?" I suggested awkwardly, after a pause. "They do convict Lady Chandos, I suppose?"

"Up to the hilt. Women are mad about letters. Gives us this other woman, too. Now our information about the numbers of the notes may be useful. Of course, the hundred Bannister got from Ferguson would go to her, so that if awkward questions concerning numbers were asked, there'd be nothing to connect the two."

"I still find it hard to believe that all Lady Chandos' misery over Dacre was mere play-acting," I persisted. "If you'd heard her, as I did, on the morning of the tragedy, standing with him by the lily-pond, telling him he was all her world...."

"Had the police arrived then?" Egerton interjected sharply.

"Yes. They'd finished the cross-examination and were searching the house. I ran into Bannister in the garden, and we saw Bradlaugh's shadow against the window of your room."

"Was he standing just there, then?"

"Yes. He was interested in some plant or other Lady Chandos was cultivating."

"And then?"

"I offered to show him the sunk garden. I didn't know, of course, that Lady Chandos was talking to Dacre there. But we came upon them suddenly."

"And stayed?"

"Yes. It would have been too pointed to have cleared out, like kids caught stealing jam."

"And after that?"

"I talked a minute to Dacre, and Lady Chandos pointed out the beauties of the place to Bannister, and then we sheered off."

"Can't you remember it in more detail than that?" He seemed irritated and a little contemptuous. So I searched my memory and dragged forth every incident I could recall connected with the occasion. When I finished Egerton stood looking at me, as if he were weighing me in the balance and finding me grievously wanting.

"I'm dumbfounded," he said candidly, when he had finished staring me out of countenance. "You've had this clue in your hands from the outset, and you've let it slide."

"What clue?"

Egerton made a gesture of despair. "Look here, Ravenswood, Rosemary's a pal of yours. She'll be needing some one to stand by her tonight as she's never needed any one all her life long—and never will again while I'm above earth. I don't know what Bremner's going to do, but I want your word that you'll go down to Dover now. and do anything you can for her. When they take that fellow, she'll be in the most damnable position conceivable. You'll go? And at once?"

"Aren't you coming?" I demanded in perplexity. It was about as easy trying to get to grips with quicksilver as follow the mazes of this fellow's mind.

"I can't," he said shortly. "I've got to go down to Freyne. Besides, I doubt if I should be much use at Dover tonight. You'll go?"

"I'll go," I promised, and without a word to Bremner he walked out of the room. An instant later we saw him tearing past in the taxi that had brought us here.

"What the devil . . . ?" Bremner began, hanging up the receiver.

I shook my head. "I don't know. I doubt if any one does know where he's concerned. You're sure it'll be all right about Bannister?"

"Yes. The arrest will be made before the boat sails. I've telephoned the docks to make doubly sure. It won't be hard to get them. And now I'm going on to Walham Green. This woman is an accessory after the crime, and I'm going to arrest her as such. Are you seeing the show through?"

"I'm going to Dover," I said, and went.

II

So Bremner and his men finished the course alone. I tell their story as I heard it later, since it falls into its place here. It was very brief.

They reached the block of buildings in Walham Green, only to find their prey was flown. The rooms she had occupied were empty and stark; their footsteps echoed forlornly on the bare boards; one picture on a rusty nail leered drunkenly at them from the wall. A basket was stuffed with odds and ends of rubbish, rags and torn papers, old stockings and empty cotton-reels. The most minute examination showed nothing in the nature of a letter from Bannister. That she must have had such letters Bremner knew from the papers he had found. He had read these on his way, and had obtained, not merely full documentary evidence of Catherine's complicity and treachery to Chandos (for Bannister had been her lover for two years), but also the receipt and a letter from Charlotte Manvers, which proved that she had been one of the gallery of women and was now his accomplice in blackmail.

"Do you remember," Bremner asked me, in telling his story, "the inexplicable death of a young girl in society a short time ago? No one knew what had happened, but she hanged herself with her own silk stockings. Here's the true story. Bannister—or this woman—had learned of an—indiscretion, let's call it—she had committed, and they were bleeding her white. She hadn't the courage, poor kid, to tell the truth to the man she loved and was going to marry. She'd done nothing actually wrong, but she'd compromised herself fatally through sheer innocence. And then, when she couldn't meet these bloodsuckers' demands any longer, she took the only way out—the way that, eventually, Bannister will take, though not of his own will."

In the bedroom of the Walham Green flat, they discovered all that Manvers had left behind of her guilty secrets. Despite the heat of the weather she had kindled a small fire in the grate, and here she had burned a quantity of papers. Most of them had been crumbled by hand to a fine black ash; all were indecipherable.

"Bannister's letters," Bremner decided. "No use to us as evidence, though. Still, we've got as much of that as we need. Let's look for the landlord."

The man in charge of the estate office on the ground floor was obviously a little nervous at the presence of Scotland Yard but he was perfectly civil. Yes, Miss Manvers had left that morning. These flats were tenable on a monthly basis, but Miss Manvers had gone out at two days' notice, paying a month's rent instead. She had paid him with a ten-pound note. No, he had not changed it yet. She had only gone early that morning. He produced it at Bremner's request. As we had expected, it was one of those Bannister had received from Ferguson.

Bremner explained the position briefly. "I shall want this," he added, pocketing the note, "but of course, you won't be the loser."

Then he went out to pick up the trail.

I heard afterwards that he found her, and she was imprisoned for a good many years. But by that time I wasn't interested in her any longer.

CHAPTER 17 THE END OF THE TRAIL

I

By sheer ill-luck I missed the quick connection to Dover, and by the time I arrived most of the work was done. I went direct to the police station to learn from them where the Bannisters might be found. But my search ended there. The arrest had actually taken place on board; there had been an ugly scene, the general impression being that Rosemary was concerned in her guardian's death. When I went to the police headquarters I found them both there.

Bannister took his losses well. No spasm of emotion twisted the muscles of his face as he stood, handcuffed, in one corner of the room. His smile was as suave as ever, his manner easy. But when he saw me a look flashed for a moment into his eyes that told me that he guessed at the part I had played in the drama.

Rosemary, colourless as paper, frozen almost to immobility, was sitting by a table in the middle of the room. When I came in she greeted me with a little cry and came over quickly.

"Alan! Tell me what it all means. First Rupert, then Miss Dennis, and now Guy. It's like a nightmare, only—I can't wake up."

"I want you to come away from here," I told her. (It was what the police authorities wanted, too.) "There are some people I know..." but she drew away from me.

"I don't understand," she said in bewildered tones. "Are you in this, too? And why Guy? That man (I suppose she meant the officer who made the arrest), said something about Catherine. I can't make head or tail of it. Nor can Guy."

"You'll understand it soon enough," I said. "For the moment this isn't a rightful place for you to be."

She laughed a little hysterically. "I'd better not go far. They might want me next. They've had three shots—or four, if it's true about Catherine. Who'll be the next?"

"There won't be any next," said a drawn voice behind us. I swung round. Egerton had come in unheard. I hadn't realised till then how close Freyne is by car to Dover. He hadn't taken any risk of trains, but had come down from town the whole journey by road. Presumably he had found what he sought at Freyne, for, for the first time, his face had that look of utter exhaustion that men of his calibre only show when they have accomplished their job and have reached the end of their tether. He was whiter than Rosemary, almost dropping with fatigue. Nothing but his indomitable will kept him on his feet.

Rosemary took two steps past me. "Is this another of your intrigues?" she whispered fiercely.

He bowed. "Since you are pleased to call it so."

"What's your plan?" she cried. "This—this absurd accusation can't hold water." He didn't waver, and a sudden fear swept into her face.

"It's ridiculous," she repeated defiantly. "All this yarn about Catherine and Guy. Isn't it, Alan? Tell me it's all some stupid bungle."

I couldn't find any words, but we didn't really need them. She glanced for a minute from me to Egerton and back. I suppose our faces revealed the truth. I hope mine did. It was easier than speech. A terrifying change came over her. She seemed literally to shrivel up; her face became haggard, her manner appalled. It is not nice to learn on your wedding night that your husband is as choice a blackguard as you would hope to find in hell.

Bannister's voice cut across the silence. "May I ask how much longer we are to be treated to these heroics?" he asked. "My wife has told you her views. I suggest that it would be more delicate to allow the matter to take its natural course. No further interference is necessary or desirable."

I touched Rosemary's arm. "Come with me," I begged her. "There are some people here—if you insist on staying in Dover for the night—who will put you up. We can discuss this further in the morning."

But Rosemary was only recovering slowly from the stunning shock of the evening's work.

"What was it the doctor said when he saw Simon that morning?" she asked. "How lonely a thing is the human soul! It's true. There was you," she glanced at Egerton, and glanced swiftly away again, "there was Simon, and he's gone; and Catherine—and Guy—— And now there's no one."

Egerton said wearily, "That's not altogether true," and the sound of his voice acted as a restorative. "Ravenswood will look after you," he went on. But she withdrew herself from both of us with a fine gesture.

"Thank you, Alan," she said, "but my place is here—with my husband," and she went across to where Bannister, manacled but triumphant, stood between two plain-clothes men.

II

So in the end Egerton went back to town alone. I was putting up at Dover, for, of course, Rosemary wasn't going to be allowed to spend the night in the prison. After some difficulty I persuaded her to come with me, and I got her a bed with the M'Intoshes, who had been my friends for twenty years. A word in Mrs M'Intosh's ear had been enough, so I had no further need to trouble on her score till dawn. Egerton was different; he insisted on going back to London. But before he went he told me the reason for his dash to Freyne.

"All along I've been puzzled about the syringe," he said. "Of course, when the plot was laid, Bannister intended to leave it somewhere in Chandos' desk. Then he discovered the tablets, and fearing that suspicion might be aroused if morphine in two forms was discovered, decided to blindfold possible pursuers by crushing the tablets, and concealing the syringe elsewhere. Directly the murder thesis was sprung on the house he saw his danger. For he had the syringe in his room—or on his person. He must have known that the first thing a detective would do would be to seal the rooms, and to search the occupants of the house. Obviously, the only safe place was the garden. But he dared not go out at that hour for fear of exciting comment. Some servant might blurt out that she'd seen Mr Bannister going down to the sunk garden—something of that sort. So he did the only thing left to him, went unostentatiously up to his room and dropped the syringe out of the window into the bed of shrubs below. Then he seized his opportunity and recovered it while Bradlaugh and his men were searching the house. You thought he was admiring the plants in the borders; he was sharp enough to comment on them, but in reality he had just secured the syringe, and was waiting to put it in some place of safety. By talking of gardening he cleverly persuaded you to suggest an excursion to the lily-pond, where Lady Chandos was waiting for him. Then you turned to Dacre and he came up to her, passing the syringe as he did so. She, being a woman of quick intellect, found in the most natural manner possible a device for dropping it to the bottom of the pond which, as she gratuitously informed you, was very deep."

"Of course," I exclaimed. "The frog!"

"Exactly. As soon as I'd heard your story I was certain that here was the answer to the riddle. So I posted hell-for-leather down to Freyne, got a couple of men and a constable from the village, and we dragged the pond and, of course, found the syringe embedded among the weeds that line the bottom. It's a bit rusty, but none the less evidence. I went back to the station, made the usual statement, signed it, had it witnessed by the bobby, and left the syringe in official hands. Then I came on here, on the off-chance that I could do some good. It's obvious that I can't. You'll hang about here till you're sure it's all well with Rosemary, won't you?"

"The M'lntoshes will look after her. I think, on the whole, she's better without any of us. We've witnessed her supreme humiliation. I don't wonder she wants to hide from the crowd of us. Poor child! She's had a pretty thorough course of disillusion during the past six weeks."

He nodded. "No doubt you're right. But that last gesture was magnificent—crazy, if you like, but magnificent. You must admit that. On my soul, for the instant I almost envied Bannister."

Then he went away rather quickly, and I sat up all night, wondering how long it would take to effect some sort of reconciliation between two of the proudest and most stubborn youngsters I had ever run up against.

III

I wasn't present at the humiliating and degrading scene of Catherine Chandos' arrest. Egerton had been a true prophet when he had said she couldn't play even her game with a straight bat.

But it was I who met Dacre on the morning of his release, and carried him back to town with me. I was planning an African expedition that autumn, as a kind of antidote to the strenuous summer I had endured, and I thought he might feel like joining me. He greeted the project with enthusiasm. He was closing down Dacre Court for a time, he said. Even if I hadn't suggested the African exploit, he wouldn't be living there. Presently, because he was incapable of further repression, he began to talk of the murder. He had, of course, seen the papers with their ghastly story, chiefly gleaned from Catherine's letters. The association between the two and their murderous plot had been revealed therein, beyond a shadow of doubt.

"He'll swing," I agreed reluctantly. "But she isn't the actual murderer. She may get off with imprisonment...."

Dacre shivered, and suddenly began to strip himself, as I suppose he had never done in his life before, and never would again. All the emotions he had kept bottled up since the war, the neurosis that had sprung, partly from shock, partly from fear and partly from his morbid relation towards Catherine, he spread out like a pedlar displaying his wares, for my benefit.

"I've known it for years," he said violently. "When she married Chandos I was certain of it. And I couldn't escape. I was like a mouse being played with by a cat. And I worshipped her, because she meant me to. But in my heart, when I had the courage to dig deep enough, I knew she was rotten. Most of the time I disbelieved it. I hated myself for even thinking such a thing—yet I knew it was true. It was like being fascinated by a great poisonous flower, lovely to look at, but deadly to touch. And yet, even when I knew that best of all, I'd be mad for her. I've seen fellows rotting with drugs or drink, and their craving was like mine. They couldn't get away. I couldn't. She didn't mean me to. If I seemed starving, she'd fling me a crust. But this last time—I didn't mean to come. What decent man could after Chandos' note? Then she asked me, and I came, like a needle to a magnet. But that night, when she turned Chandos' soul sick within him, I swore I'd shake myself free. It was horrible. And the next day she tossed her reputation away as lightly as a wind tosses thistledown, and stood up in front of them all and defended me. I didn't think of anything, but that she cared enough—so much that Chandos faded out of the picture. . . . Only after the arrest I began to grow sane. I saw that what she'd committed me to was a worse thing than the crime for which I was arrested. But she didn't think of it like that. One was criminal and the other wasn't. That was the moment of my release." He broke off, panting and sweating. Presently he said, in a slow, dead voice, as though the flames had died out and this was the last faint gray curl of smoke rising out of the ashes, "Ten years—and I'm free at last. My God! Free!"

That was the last word he spoke till we reached town.

CHAPTER 18 THE SCALES ADJUSTED

I

The trial took place in early September, and by the time it was over I felt that both Dacre and I had earned our holiday. To begin with, Rosemary insisted on staying in town and keeping up a constant communication with Bannister. Egerton she steadfastly refused to meet. On her own account, she discovered a brilliant (and slightly unscrupulous) lawyer, who undertook Bannister's defence, Rosemary paying the fee from her private purse. As often as the regulations permitted she visited the fellow in his cell and carried out various commissions for him.

"I must, Alan," she said steadily, when I remonstrated with her. "I'm his wife. I've sworn to stand by him for better or worse, and I can't back out just because it happens to be worse from the very beginning."

"But the position's hopeless," I reminded her gently.

"I dare say, but I should never forgive myself if I didn't do everything possible. There's no one else, you see. You'll all be giving evidence against him."

"You won't be asked for evidence," I said.

"I should refuse, anyway. They couldn't force me. No wife has to appear against her husband."

I was amazed (and Egerton very much less so) at her courage; she must be aware that supposing her lawyer got Bannister off the extreme penalty she'd practically be a widow for the next twenty years. It's only in novels that decrees of nullity shower round the heroine's head like leaves off an autumnal bough.

"I suppose," she went on, avoiding my eyes, "you're making all the arrangements for Catherine. That's nothing to do with me."

I perjured myself hastily. Truth to tell, I hadn't thought much about Catherine. What with Rosemary, Dacre, and Egerton my hands had been pretty full. However, clearly I should have to take the matter over. I had been Catherine's confidante throughout. I smiled wryly to think what a jury would make of my evidence. If I couldn't show my utter ignorance of her motives I might yet find myself suspect of complicity.

I got the necessary permit without much trouble. Catherine's appearance shocked me profoundly. I had expected something rather appalling, but not the wasted woman with the glassy eyes and ravaged face who rose slowly to meet me. She was so thin that she seemed like a skeleton hung with clothes.

"Couldn't you have spared me even this?" she whispered. "Must you add to my humiliations?"

I explained awkwardly that I wanted to make adequate arrangements for her defence.

She lifted thin, aimless hands. "What's the use? We can't deny anything now."

"All the same, a lawyer might make a difference," I urged. (All the difference, in fact, between life and death.)

Catherine shook her head. She was so wasted that it seemed to droop loosely on her thin neck. "No, it's too late now. Do you think I'd be afraid to die? I'd be glad to get out—but not that way. Alan, you must help me for the last time. I can't go through that. Couldn't you . . . ?"

I said abruptly that I couldn't. I didn't propose to find myself in the felon's dock for murder.

"There must be some way," Catherine ran on, clasping her hands feverishly. "It was bad enough before, but now. . . . It's Rupert, Alan. I can't face him. He believed in me for so long, and I just—used him as a decoy. Simon used to say the only unpardonable sin was exploitation, and I did that. But I never meant him to be arrested. You must believe that. Guy didn't tell me that that was part of his plan. Suicide we said—we thought it would never be known. But I didn't mean him to imitate Rupert's step, put the seal in the room, the letter in the blotter. He didn't tell me he was going to do that. And when I heard I had to find some excuse for Rupert on the spur of the minute. I hadn't time to think of anything except that he'd been with me. And when he denied it—well, that didn't matter. Any man would, and no one took any notice of him. But afterwards it grew worse. When they took him away. . . . Ever since then I've been wondering what I could do if they brought him in guilty. It's been—hell—and I couldn't stir a finger. It wasn't all play-acting, Alan. Afterwards —when I understood that Simon had known all about Guy and found out how vile Guy was—then I'd have killed myself to undo the awful thing we'd done. I was mad, of course. . . . But it was too late. I just had to go on playing the game—a poor game it turned out. Alan, do you think when I'm dead I shall be able to forget?" Her voice was rising, becoming shrill and terrified. I did my best to soothe her, but the fear was in her soul. She dared not face life because of what she knew about herself, and she was afraid of death for the same reason. I thought of various things. Of the position in which she had put herself for Dacre's sake; of the letters Manvers had held and the price Catherine had had to pay; of all she must have endured when Bannister's engagement was announced. There had never been one moment since the commission of the crime that she had known peace or security. It was impossible not to pity her a little. . . .

II

The trial was, of course, a *cause célèbre*. Both Chandos and Bannister were too well known for the thing to pass off unnoticed. Rosemary and I went down to the court daily, but neither Egerton nor Dacre put in an appearance except when they were in the witness-box.

Bannister seemed unmoved throughout. His hands never

shook either when he was in the witness-box himself or when he waited, behind the scenes, for the jury's decision.

Catherine, on the other hand, was distraught. She admitted everything, and her lawyer walked out of the court in disgust the moment the verdict was announced. I saw Bannister glance at her once or twice; he was contemptuous of her attitude, but when his eyes rested on the girl who had married him, and stuck by him ever since, to her own detriment, they were full of a genuine and deep-seated admiration. Rosemary had done herself little good by her loyalty. The general impression here also was that she was implicated in the murder, and ugly looks were cast at her, as the case progressed. I don't think Rosemary noticed them.

The jury were out of the court a very short time. They brought in the verdict every one expected, wilful murder against Catherine and Bannister, with a recommendation to mercy in the former case. Bannister heard the capital sentence without emotion, declared quietly that he had nothing to say and left the court. Catherine fainted; subsequently she was reprieved, but I doubt if the jury's recommendation was as merciful as they imagined.

No one attempted to get up a reprieve for Bannister, nor did he appeal. As Egerton had prophesied, he could play his game with a straight bat. Rosemary went to see him for the last time, at his request, on the day before the execution. I think the only thing that moved him throughout the whole of that time was her attitude.

"My God, Rosemary!" he said as she bade him goodbye, "you know how to lose!"

At noon the next day, when there was no longer any need for that desperate courage that had upheld her hitherto, reaction set in, and she collapsed utterly. Dacre and I postponed our African expedition.

"I promised Egerton," I explained.

"Egerton be damned!" said Dacre gruffly, "you'd have stayed anyway. So should I!"

III

The general excitement of the Bannister trial, and his participation in it, had cost Egerton the Cattering constituency. But six months after Bannister's execution the Liberals offered him a north-country seat, and on the day after his name appeared at the head of the poll, with sixteen hundred votes in hand, he came to see me at my rooms. I congratulated him sincerely enough, though his political views were not mine. I was disappointed to find him so fit; I suppose I had hoped to see something more of the tormented lover. But when Rosemary's name was mentioned, as it was bound to be, I got all the satisfaction I wanted.

"She's going abroad next week," I told him. "Mrs M'lntosh wants to get her away from this country altogether. She has an idea that she'll regain an interest in life in a new atmosphere. At present she's absolutely limp."

"Doesn't sound like Rosemary," Egerton commented, knitting his brows. He seemed hesitating on the brink of some confidence and suddenly, without warning, he broke into a spate of self-recrimination.

"It's been my fault, start to finish," he said. "I ought to be flayed alive for letting the matter go as far as I did. If I'd gone straight to the Yard, when we discovered the discrepancy between the typewriters, this ghastly marriage would never have been possible."

I agreed awkwardly. "Bannister," he went on meditatively, and I thought morbidly, "had his points. He was a fine loser. That's one reason why Rosemary turned to him. Still, I find it difficult even now to believe that any woman could have preferred him to Chandos, the finest man of his generation. I suppose they told you how I ran up against him?"

"Yes. Lady Chandos did."

"Turning-point of my life," he went on. "Oh, I don't mean his lending a hand. Scores of men would have done that, seeing a young fool in a devil of a mess with such a woman. But Chandos believed me. He knew I visited at Daubney's house, and he knew that, though I'd made a damned fool of myself, I wasn't cad enough to eat his salt and intrigue with his wife simultaneously. It was that that pulled me through, not the helping hand to which every one else refers. He was the only one who did believe my side of the story at the time, and probably ever since."

A clear, but very low voice behind us said, "I believe it, Scott."

We swung round, amazed. Rosemary was standing in the doorway. "I had to come up," she explained. "Mrs M'Tntosh is taking me abroad with her next week but I had to see Scott first. I met Rupert this morning, and he told me I should find him here."

She looked up at Egerton nervously, but he didn't offer to help her, for all she was so white and exhausted. She'd had a pretty bad time. Perhaps, though, he couldn't. He was standing with his hands in his pockets, his favourite attitude when his feelings were deeply stirred. For an instant she hesitated; then, because she had never been one to shirk her fences, she drove her spurs into the steed of her courage and soared over.

"I don't suppose it makes much difference to you now what I think," she said, meeting his eyes squarely, "but I couldn't have hated you so much when I believed the general version of the Daubney case if I hadn't loved you so much first that it maddened me to think of your being stained by such a story. Now, of course, I can see how vile it was of me even to have believed it for an hour. But, Catherine—and Guy——" she stopped, and gathering herself together, began again, "I don't know when I'll see you again, or if I ever shall. And it isn't any good apologising now for an awful thing like that. But—will you shake hands? And at least you can forget. It can't mean very much to you."

She held out her hand to him. I saw her wince as he took it and drove all the blood out of her numbing fingers. He was a head and a half taller than she, and he stood looking down at her, trying to conquer himself sufficiently to speak. At last he said, in a voice that was altogether shaken out of its customary calm,

"It's the only thing that matters now—that you and Chandos..." he broke off, incapable for the moment of further speech. Then, as she opened her lips, he went on quickly, "We'll make a bargain, Rosemary, you and I, and Ravenswood shall be our witness, because he has been with us from the beginning." (His conversation frequently had a scriptural flavour.) "We'll never speak of this again in all our lives together. It's finished. God knows you've footed a pretty heavy bill."

Rosemary's answer was to half-turn towards me and say, "Alan, dear, you've got a most wonderful hall. I don't believe you half appreciate it."

I was already at the door. As I opened it Scott Egerton, without bothering to lift his head, put in, "You'll see us through this, old chap, as you have through all the rest? We shan't delay you many days." (For Dacre and I were due to sail the following week).

I swerved round, caught a swift glimpse of his face, and shut the door silently.

*

I was still in the hall when Dacre came in. I told him what had happened.

"Thought as much," he commented. "Met Rosemary this morning, you know. How long will it hold us up?"

"Not more than a fortnight, I should imagine. It'll be a quiet enough affair. They've both had enough of publicity. But Egerton's also had enough of waiting." (As a matter of fact, we caught our boat after all, for Rosemary and Egerton were married at the beginning of the following week and later came down to see us off.)

"Well," said Dacre solemnly, "Rosemary's a good sort, and the straightest I've ever met, but sooner him than me. Ravenswood, can you realise that in a month or so we shall be camping in acres and acres of sand? Nice, quiet, empty sand with a few Arabs and camels and thorn-bushes to relieve the monotony, and no women for miles—and miles...?"

But I remembered that half-glance I had had of Egerton's face before I shut the door, and I thought that here as usual there was a good deal to be said for his point of view.

Made in United States
North Haven, CT
03 February 2024

48253052R00129